FOREV
A

(THE INN AT

SOPHIE LOVE

ISBN: 978-1-63291-880-2

BOOKS BY SOPHIE LOVE

THE INN AT SUNSET HARBOR
FOR NOW AND FOREVER (Book #1)
FOREVER AND FOR ALWAYS (Book #2)
FOREVER, WITH YOU (Book #3)

CHAPTER ONE

"Good morning."

Emily stirred and opened her eyes. The sight that greeted her was the most beautiful she could ever have hoped for: Daniel, framed by the crisp white bedding, a halo of morning sunshine kissing his tousled hair. She took a deep, satisfied breath, wondering how her life had aligned so perfectly. After so many years of hardship, it felt like fate had finally decided to give her a break.

"Morning." She smiled back, yawning.

She snuggled back down under the covers, feeling cozy, warm, and more relaxed than ever. The quiet calmness of a Sunset Harbor morning was in such stark contrast to the busy bustle of her old life in New York City. Emily could certainly get used to this, to the sound of breaking waves in the distance, to the smell of the ocean, to the gorgeous man lying beside her in bed.

She got up and went over to the large French doors that led out onto the balcony, opening them so she could feel the warm sunshine on her skin. The ocean sparkled in the distance and rays of light illuminated the master bedroom behind her. It had been a dusty ruin when Emily arrived six months ago. Now it was a beautiful cove of tranquility, with white walls and bedding, soft carpeting, a gorgeous four-poster bed, and carefully restored antique bedside tables. With the sun on her face, Emily felt that for once everything was perfect.

"So are you ready for your big day?" Daniel said from the bed.

Emily frowned, her head still too muggy from sleep to comprehend.

"Big day?"

Daniel smirked.

"First customer. Remember?"

Emily's thoughts took a moment to click into place. But then she remembered that she had her very first guest, Mr. Kapowski, sleeping in the room down the hall. The house she'd been restoring for six months had been transformed from a home into a business, and that meant she had breakfast to make.

"What time is it?" she asked.

"Eight," Daniel replied.

Emily froze.

"Eight?"

"Yes."

1

"NO! I overslept!" Emily cried, running back inside from the balcony. She grabbed the alarm clock and shook it angrily. "You were supposed to wake me up at six, you stupid thing!"

She slammed it back down on the bedside table, then rushed to the chest of drawers to find some clothes, flinging sweaters and pants all over the place. Nothing looked professional enough; she'd thrown out all of her office wear from her old life in New York, and everything she owned now was practical.

"Calm down," Daniel chuckled from the bed. "It's okay."

"How is it okay?" Emily cried, hopping around with one leg in her pants. "Breakfast started at seven!"

"And it only takes five minutes to poach an egg," Daniel added.

Emily froze on the spot, half dressed, her face drawn like she'd seen a ghost. "You think he'll want his eggs poached? I haven't a clue how to poach an egg!"

Rather than calming her, Daniel's words only panicked her further. She wrenched a crumpled lilac sweater from the drawer and pulled it over her head, the static making her hair instantly frizz.

"Where's my mascara?" Emily cried as she rushed around. "And will you stop laughing at me?" she added, glaring angrily at Daniel. "This isn't funny. I have a guest. A paying guest! And nothing but sneakers to put on my feet. Why did I throw out all my heels?"

Daniel's stifled chuckles became full-on belly laughs.

"I'm not laughing at you," he managed to say. "I'm laughing because I'm happy. Because being with you makes me happy."

Emily paused, his words striking a chord deep inside of her. She looked over at him, lying languorously like a God in her bed. His was a face you couldn't stay mad at for long.

Daniel broke their gaze. Though Emily was used to it now, to Daniel clamming up whenever he got too close to his own emotions, it still distressed her. Her own feelings were so obvious as to be practically transparent. That she wore her heart on her sleeve, Emily was in no doubt.

But he sometimes left her floundering. She was never certain with him, and it reminded her almost too painfully of her previous relationships, of the unsteadiness she felt within them, like she was standing on the deck of a rocking boat at sea, destined to never find her sea legs. She didn't want history to repeat itself with Daniel. She wanted it to be different with him. But experience had taught her that getting what you wanted in life was a rare occurrence.

2

She turned back to the dresser, quiet now, and put two silver studs in her ears.

"That will have to do," she said, her gaze flicking away from Daniel's reflection in the mirror and to herself, her expression reconfigured from a panicked girl into a determined businesswoman.

Emily strode purposefully out of her room to find everything silent. The upstairs corridor was stunning now, with beautiful wall sconces and an amazing chandelier that caught the morning sunshine and refracted shards of light everywhere. The wooden floors had been polished to perfection, adding a rustic yet glamorous touch.

Emily looked down at the door at the end, to the room that had previously belonged to her and Charlotte. Restoring that room had been the hardest thing of all because she'd felt like she was erasing her sister. But all of Charlotte's things were sitting neatly in a special place in the attic, and Emily's friend Serena, a local artist, had created some amazing artwork out of her sister's clothes. Still, she felt a squirming sensation in her stomach knowing that there was a stranger sleeping on the other side of that door, a stranger to whom she now needed to serve breakfast. In all Emily's imaginings about transforming the house into a B&B, she'd never really daydreamed about what that might actually be like, look like, or feel like. She suddenly felt woefully underprepared, like a child pretending to be a grown-up.

Ensuring she was as quiet as possible, Emily padded along the corridor toward the staircase. The new cream carpet felt luxurious beneath her feet. She couldn't help but gaze at it adoringly. The transformation of the house had been a real wonder to behold. There was still work to be done—the third floor in particular was an absolute mess, with rooms she hadn't even set foot in yet; not to mention the outbuildings that contained an abandoned swimming pool, along with a whole plethora of boxes to sort. But what she had achieved thus far, with a little help from the friendly Sunset Harbor locals, still amazed her. The house felt like a friend to her now, one that still had secrets to share. In fact, there was one key in particular that was proving to be a mystery to her. No matter how hard she tried, she could not find what it unlocked. She'd checked everything from desk drawers to wardrobe doors but had still not found it.

Emily went down the long staircase, its banisters now polished and glistening, the fluffy carpet looking resplendent, the brass runners setting off the colors perfectly. But just as she was admiring everything, she noticed that there was a blemish on the carpet—a smudgy, muddy footprint. It was clearly from a man's boot.

Emily paused on the bottom step. *Daniel needs to be more careful when he's clomping around,* she thought.

But then she realized the footprint was pointing away, heading toward the front door. Which meant it had come from upstairs. But if Daniel was still in bed, then the only way the footprint could have gotten there was from her guest, Mr. Kapowski.

Emily rushed to the front door and flung it open. Just the day before, Mr. Kapowski had driven up the newly formed driveway in his estate car and parked. But now his car was gone.

She couldn't believe it.

He had left.

CHAPTER TWO

Panicking, Emily rushed back into the house.

"Daniel!" she cried up the stairs. "Mr. Kapowski's gone! He left because I wasn't up in time to make him breakfast!"

Daniel appeared at the top of the stairs wearing only his pajama bottoms, his broad shoulders and muscular chest on display. His hair was a mess, giving him the air of a hurried schoolboy.

"He probably just went to Joe's," he said, trotting down the steps toward her. "You were going on about how amazing the waffles were, if you recall."

"But *I'm* supposed to make him breakfast!" Emily cried. "It's a B *and B*, not just a B!"

Daniel reached the landing and swept Emily up into his arms, holding her gently around her waist. "Maybe he didn't realize what the second B stood for. Thought it stood for bath. Or bananas," he joked. He pressed a kiss into her neck but Emily batted him away and wriggled out of the embrace.

"Daniel, stop fooling around!" she cried. "This is serious. He's my first ever guest and I wasn't awake in time to make him breakfast."

Daniel shook his head and rolled his eyes with mocking affection.

"It's no big deal. He'll just be having breakfast down by the ocean instead. He's on vacation, remember?"

"But there's an ocean view from my porch," Emily stammered, her voice growing thin. She sank down onto the bottom step, feeling small, like a child who'd been put on the naughty step, then dropped her head in her hands. "I'm a horrible host."

Daniel rubbed her shoulders. "That's not true. You're just a little unsteady on your feet right now. Everything's strange and new. But you're doing fine. Okay?"

He said the last word sternly, almost paternally. Emily couldn't help but be comforted. She looked up at him.

"Do you want me poach *you* an egg at least?" she asked.

"That would be delightful." Daniel smiled. He cupped her face in his hands and pressed a kiss onto her lips.

Together they went into the kitchen. The noise of the door opening stirred Mogsy the dog and her pup, Rain, from their slumber in the utility room, just the other side of the barn doors. Emily knew that keeping the dogs out of the kitchen and any parts of the house she needed as the B&B was an absolute must if she didn't want to get closed down for health and safety reasons immediately, but she felt bad confining the dogs to such a small portion of the house. She reminded herself that it was a temporary situation. She'd been able to have four of Mogsy's five pups adopted by her friends in town, but Rain, the weak runt, was a harder sell, and no one seemed even remotely interested in taking the mama, who was, to put it gently, an ugly mutt.

Once the dogs were let outside and fed, Emily went back into the kitchen. In the meantime, Daniel had managed to pop out into the garden to fetch this morning's eggs from Lola and Lolly, the chickens, and brew a pot of coffee. Emily took a mug gratefully and breathed in the aroma, then went over to the large Arga stove— another relic of her father's she'd had restored—and got to work practicing making poached eggs.

Of all the rooms in the house, the kitchen was one of Emily's favorites. The poor room had been ravished by time and abandonment when she'd first arrived, then a storm had whipped through it causing further damage, and *then* the toaster had blown up and caused a fire. The smoke damage had been far more destructive than the actual fire; that had only damaged a shelf and consumed some cookbooks, whereas the smoke had managed to permeate every crack and crevice, leaving streaks of black and the odor of burnt plastic wherever it had touched.

In just six short months, everything that could have gone wrong with the room had. But after some grueling late nights toiling away, it had now finally been re-re-restored and looked charming, with its retro fridge and original white Victorian Belfast basin, and its black marble work surfaces.

"Turns out," Emily said, plunking her fifth attempt at a poached egg on Daniel's plate, "that I'm not such a horrible cook after all."

"See?" Daniel said, cutting into the white of the egg and letting the golden yolk spill across his toast. "I told you. You have to listen to me more often."

Emily smiled, enjoying Daniel's gentle humor. Ben, her ex, had never made her laugh like Daniel did. He'd never been able to comfort her in her moments of panic either. With Daniel it was like nothing was ever too big to handle. Be it storm or fire, he always made her feel like everything was okay, was manageable. His steadiness was one of the most appealing things about him. He could calm and soothe her in the same way looking out at the ocean calmed her. But she was still never certain where he stood, whether he was feeling what she was feeling. She felt that their relationship was like a riptide, one they couldn't control even if they wanted to.

"So," Daniel said, munching happily on his breakfast, "after we've eaten, we should probably start getting ready."

"Getting ready for what?" Emily asked, sipping on her second mug of steaming black coffee.

"It's the Memorial Day Parade," Daniel said.

Emily vaguely remembered attending the parade as a child and wanted to see it again, but she'd already messed up enough today to allow herself a trip.

"I have too much to do here. I need to make up the guest bedroom."

"Already done," Daniel replied. "I fixed up the room while you were with the dogs."

"You did?" Emily asked suspiciously. "Did you replace the towels?"

Daniel nodded.

"And the mini shampoos?"

"Yup."

"What about the little sachets of coffee and sugar?"

Daniel raised an eyebrow. "Everything that needed to be replaced was replaced. I made the bed—and before you say anything, yes, I do know how to make a bed, I've lived alone for years. Everything is ready for him when he returns. So, are you coming to the parade?"

Emily shook her head. "I need to be here for when Mr. Kapowski gets back."

"He doesn't need babysitting."

Emily chewed her lip. She was nervous about her first guest and desperate to do a good job. If she couldn't make this work, she'd be returning to New York with her tail between her legs, probably to sleep on Amy's couch, or worse, in her mom's spare room.

"But what if he needs something. More pillows? Or—"

"—more bananas?" Daniel interrupted with a smirk.

Emily sighed, defeated. Daniel was right. Mr. Kapowski wouldn't be expecting her to wait on him hand and foot. If anything, he would probably prefer her not to interfere too much. He was on vacation, after all. Most people wanted some peace and quiet.

"Come on," Daniel urged. "It will be fun."

"All right," Emily said, relenting. "I'll come."

Everywhere Emily looked she saw American flags. Her vision had become a kaleidoscope of stars and stripes, causing her to gasp in wonder. Flags hung in every store window, in knitted bunting strung from lamppost to lamppost. There were even some pinned to the backs of the benches. And that was nothing compared to the number of flags being waved by passersby. Everyone who strolled along the sidewalk seemed to have one.

"Daddy," Emily said, looking up at her father. "Can I have a flag too?"

The tall man smiled down at her. "Of course you can, Emily Jane."

"And me, and me!" a little voice piped up.

Emily turned to see her sister, Charlotte, her bright purple scarf wrapped around her neck, so mismatched with her ladybug boots. She was just a toddler, barely able to keep her balance.

They followed their father, both girls holding tightly to one of his hands, as they went with him across the street and into a small store that sold homemade pickles and relishes in jars.

"Well, hello, Roy." The lady behind the counter beamed. Then she grinned at the two little girls. "Up for the holidays?"

"No one does Memorial Day like Sunset Harbor," her father replied in his easygoing friendliness. "Two flags for the girls, please, Karen."

The lady fetched some flags from behind the counter. "Why don't we make it three?" she said. "Don't forget about yourself!"

"What about four?" Emily said. "We shouldn't forget about Mommy either."

Roy's jaw stiffened and Emily knew right away that she'd said the wrong thing. Mommy wouldn't want a flag. Mommy hadn't even come with them to Sunset Harbor for their weekend trip. It was just the three of them. Again. It seemed to be the three of them more and more often these days.

"Two will be plenty," her dad replied a little stiffly. "It's just for the kids really."

The woman behind the counter handed the girls a flag each, her friendliness replaced by an embarrassed kind of awkwardness in her realization that she'd accidentally stepped across some unspoken, invisible line.

Emily watched as her father paid the woman and thanked her, noting how his smile was forced now, how his posture was stiffer.

She wished she hadn't said anything about Mommy. She looked at the flag in her gloved grasp, suddenly feeling less like celebrating.

Emily gasped, finding herself back on the Sunset Harbor high street with Daniel. She shook her head, dislodging the swirling memories. This was not the first time she had experienced a sudden return of a lost memory, but the experience still shook her to the core.

"Are you okay?" Daniel said, touching her arm lightly, his expression concerned.

"Yes," Emily replied, but her voice sounded stunned. She tried to smile but only managed to weakly raise the corners of her mouth. She hadn't told Daniel about the way her childhood memories were returning to her in fragments; she didn't want to scare him away.

Determined not to let the intrusive memories ruin her enjoyment of the day, Emily threw herself into the celebrations. Many years may have passed since she was last here, but Emily was still in awe of the spectacle of it all. She marveled at the way the small town took celebrations and ran with them. One of the things she was growing to love the most about Sunset Harbor was its traditions. She had a feeling Memorial Day was going to become another holiday she loved.

"Hi, Emily!" Raj Patel called from the other side of the street. He was walking along with his wife, Dr. Sunita Patel, two people whom Emily now considered friends.

Emily waved to them and then said to Daniel, "Oh look. There's Birk and Bertha. And is that baby Katy in the stroller with Jason and Vanessa?" She pointed at the gas station owner and his disabled wife. Beside them stood their son, the firefighter who had saved Emily's kitchen from a blaze. He and his wife had recently had their first child, a girl called Katy, and had taken one of Emily's stray puppies as a gift for her. "We should go and say hello," Emily said, wanting to speak to her friends.

"In a minute," Daniel said, nudging her with his shoulder. "The parade's coming."

Emily looked down the street as the local high school's marching band lined up, ready to begin the procession. The drum began to beat and was swiftly followed by the sound of the brass instruments playing "When the Saints Go Marching In." Emily watched, delighted, as the band marched past. Behind them were cheerleaders in matching red, white, and blue ensembles. They back-flipped and high-kicked their way along the road.

Next came a troop of face-painted kindergarteners, chubby-cheeked and cherubic. Emily felt a small pang watching them.

9

Having children had never been a huge priority for her—she hadn't exactly been in a rush to become a mother considering how abysmal her relationship with her own was—but now, watching the kids in the parade, Emily realized that something had changed within her. There was a new desire there, a small yearning tugging at her. She looked across at Daniel and wondered whether it was something he felt too, whether the sight of the adorable toddlers made him feel the same way. As always, his expression was unreadable.

The parade continued on. Next up was a group of tough-looking women from the local roller derby jumping and racing around on their skates, followed by a couple of stilt-walkers and a large float carrying a papier-mâché replica of the Abraham Lincoln statue.

"Emily, Daniel," a voice came from behind. It was Mayor Hansen, flanked by his aide, Marcella, who looked more than a little harried. "Are you enjoying our local festivities?" Mayor Hansen asked. "It's not your first year if I recall, but perhaps the first you'll be able to remember."

He chuckled innocently, but Emily squirmed. She tried to put on a calm and happy demeanor.

"You're right. Sadly, I don't recall having come here as a child, but I'm certainly enjoying myself now. What about you, Marcella?" she added, trying to get the attention off of her. "Is this your first year?"

Marcella gave one decisive, efficient nod, then went back to her clipboard.

"Don't mind her." Mayor Hansen chuckled. "She's a workaholic."

Marcella's gaze flicked up just briefly, but it was long enough for Emily to read the frustration contained within her eyes. Clearly the mayor's laidback attitude frustrated her. Emily could empathize with Marcella. She'd been the same just a mere six months ago; too serious, too stressed, fueled by little more than caffeine and a fear of failure. Looking at Marcella was like holding up a mirror to her younger self. Emily's only hope for her was that she learned to unwind, that Sunset Harbor would help her to uncoil her tightly wound springs, even if only a little.

"Anyway," Mayor Hansen said, "back to the grindstone. I have medals to give out, don't I, Marcella? Award ceremony for the egg and spoon race or something."

"The Under Fives Olympics," Marcella said with an exhalation.

"That's the one," Mayor Hansen replied, and the two of them disappeared into the crowd.

Daniel smiled. "It's impossible not to fall in love with this crazy town," he said, slinging his arm around Emily.

She snuggled into him, feeling safe and protected. Together they watched a conga line go by, waving at their friends as they passed: Cynthia from the bookstore with her bright orange hair and mismatched clothing, Charles and Barbara Bradshaw from the fish shop, Parker from the organic fruit and vegetable wholesalers.

Just then, Emily spotted someone amongst the crowds who made her blood run cold. Dressed in checkered golfing pants and a lime green sweater that barely covered his portly belly, stood Trevor Mann.

"Don't look now," she grumbled, grabbing Daniel's hand for security. "But Mr. Sneery Neighbor's joined the party."

Daniel, of course, immediately looked over. Like he had some kind of sixth sense, Trevor immediately noticed. He glanced at them both, his dark eyes instantly sparkling with mischief.

Emily grimaced. "I told you not to look!" she chastised Daniel as Trevor walked toward them.

"You know there's an unwritten law," Daniel hissed back, "that says if you say 'don't look now' to someone, they're going to look."

It was too late to escape. Trevor Mann was upon them, emerging through the crowd like some horrible mustached beast.

"Oh no," Emily said, groaning.

"Emily," Trevor said in his pretend friendly voice, "you haven't forgotten about those back taxes you owe on your house, have you? Because I certainly haven't."

"The mayor gave me an extension," Emily replied. "You were in the meeting, Trevor, I'm surprised you missed it."

"I don't care whether Mayor Hansen said there's no rush in paying them back, it's not up to him. It's up to the bank. And I've been in touch with them to tell them all about your *illegal* occupation of the house and the *illegal* business you're now running from it."

"You're a jerk," Daniel said, protectively squaring up to Trevor.

"Leave it," Emily said, resting a hand on his arm. The last thing she needed was for Daniel to lose his temper.

Trevor smirked. "Mayor Hansen's extension won't last forever and certainly won't hold up in any legal sense. And I'm going to do everything in my power to make sure your B&B sinks and never floats again."

CHAPTER THREE

Emily watched as Trevor marched away into the throng of people.

As soon as he was gone, Daniel turned to Emily, a look of deep concern on his face. "Are you okay?"

Emily couldn't help herself. She sank against his broad chest, pressing her face into his shirt. "What am I going to do?" she gasped. "The taxes will ruin my business before it's even begun."

"No way," Daniel said. "I won't let that happen. Trevor Mann never showed any interest in your property until you showed up and turned it into something covetable. He's just jealous of how much better your house is than his."

Emily tried to laugh at his joke but could only manage a weak chortle. The thought of leaving Daniel and moving back to New York as a failure weighed heavily on her mind.

"He's right, though," Emily said. "This B&B will never work."

"Don't talk like that," Daniel said. "Everything will be okay. I believe in you."

"You do?" Emily said. "Because I hardly believe in myself."

"Well, maybe now is the time to start."

Emily looked up into Daniel's eyes. His earnest expression made her feel like maybe she could really do it.

"Hey," Daniel said, his eyes suddenly twinkling mischievously. "I have something I want to show you."

Daniel didn't seem discouraged by her glumness. He grabbed her hand and pulled her through the crowd, leading her in the direction of the marina. Together they went down to the docks.

"Ta-da!" Daniel exclaimed, gesturing to the beautifully restored boat bobbing in the water.

The last time Emily had seen the boat it had been barely seaworthy. Now it was glistening like brand new.

"I can't believe it," she stammered. "You fixed the boat?"

Daniel nodded. "Yup. I put a lot of sweat and effort into it."

"I can tell," Emily said.

She remembered how Daniel had told her that he'd reached some kind of mental barrier with restoring the boat, that he didn't know why but he felt unable to work on it. Seeing it now made Emily beyond proud, not just because of how beautifully he'd restored it but because he'd managed to work through whatever issues had been holding him back. She returned his smile, feeling a tingle of happiness inside of her.

But at the same time, she felt tinged with sadness, because here was yet another form of transportation that could take him away from her. From his long motorcycle rides up in the cliffs, to his journeys to neighboring cities in his truck, Daniel was forever on the move. That he wanted to see the world, explore, was so evident to her as to be beyond doubt. She knew that sooner or later, Daniel would need to leave Sunset Harbor. Whether she would leave with him when the time came was something Emily had not yet resolved in her mind.

Daniel gave her a coy nudge. "I should say thank you."

"Why?" Emily said.

"For the motor."

It had been Emily who'd bought him the new motor, as a thank-you for all the help he'd given her getting the B&B ready, as well as an attempt to encourage him to restore the boat.

"No problem," Emily said, wondering now if the gift would backfire on her. If in restoring the boat, Daniel's itch to up and leave would be ignited.

"So," Daniel said, gesturing to the boat, "as a thank-you, I think you should accompany me on its maiden voyage."

"Oh!" Emily said, startled at the proposition. "You want to go on a boat ride? Now?" She didn't mean to sound so shocked.

"Unless you don't want to," Daniel said, rubbing his neck awkwardly. "I just thought we could have a date."

"Yeah, sure," Emily said.

Daniel hopped down into the boat and held his hand out. Emily took it and allowed him to guide her down. The vessel rocked beneath her, making her wobble.

Daniel got the motor running and powered the boat out of the harbor. They crossed the glittering ocean. Emily took deep breaths of the ocean air, watching as Daniel steered them across the water. He looked so at home steering the boat, just like how his motorbike seemed to become an extension of himself. Daniel was the kind of man who suited perpetual motion, and as she looked at him now, Emily saw how alive and happy he became while in the pursuit of adventure.

The thought made her even more melancholy. Daniel's desire to explore the world was more than just a dream; it was a necessity. There was no way he would be able to stay in Sunset Harbor for much longer. She hadn't decided how long she was sticking around either. Perhaps their relationship was doomed. Maybe it was only ever going to be a fleeting thing, a perfect moment captured in time. The thought made Emily's stomach roil with despair.

"What's wrong?" Daniel asked. "You're not seasick, are you?"

"Maybe a little," Emily lied.

"Well, we're nearly there," he added, pointing ahead.

Emily glanced up and saw that they were heading toward a tiny island upon which sat little other than a couple of trees and an abandoned lighthouse. Emily sat up, suddenly surprised.

"OH MY GOD!" she cried.

"What is it?" Daniel asked, panic in his tone.

"My dad had a painting of this island in our house in New York!"

"Are you sure?"

"One hundred percent! I don't believe it! I never realized it was a painting of a real place."

Daniel's eyes widened. He seemed just as surprised by the coincidence as Emily was.

Her worries washed away by the unexpected surprise, Emily quickly removed her sneakers and socks. She barely waited for the boat to run aground before she hopped out. Waves lapped at her shins. The water was cold but she barely felt it. She ran across the water, onto the wet sandy beach, then a little further still. She stopped and held her hands up to create a rectangle of space between her fingers and thumbs and closed one eye. She maneuvered herself a little so that the lighthouse was to the right, the sun beside it, and the vast ocean stretching away on the other side. That was it! The exact angle of the painting that had been in her family home!

It didn't surprise Emily that her dad would own such a painting. He was obsessed with antiques—including art pieces—but what did surprise Emily was the fact that the painting had made it to their family home. Her mom had always been very good about keeping their Sunset Harbor life and their New York life separate, as though she could only entertain her husband's silly hobbies for two weeks of the year, and only as long as it was out of sight, not encroaching in any way on her perfectly clean, crisp home. So how on earth had he managed to get her to agree to put up the painting of the lighthouse in the family home? Maybe because it was camouflaged as an imaginary place she'd never realized the painting was actually depicting a part of Sunset Harbor? Emily smiled to herself, wondering if her father had in fact been so cunning.

"Hey," Daniel said, pulling her back to the moment. She turned to see him lugging a basket across the wet sand toward her. "You ran off!"

"Sorry," Emily replied, rushing forward to help him carry it. "What's in this thing? It weighs a ton."

Together they brought the hamper onto the beach and Daniel unclasped the buckles holding the lid down. He removed a tartan blanket and laid it across the sand.

"My lady," he said.

Emily laughed and sat down on the blanket. Daniel began to unload different foods from the hamper, including cheeses and fruits, then a large bottle of champagne and two crystal flutes.

"Champagne!" Emily exclaimed. "What's the occasion?"

Daniel shrugged. "No occasion in particular. Just thought we should celebrate your first guest."

"Don't remind me," Emily said with a groan.

Daniel popped the cork of the champagne and poured them each a glass.

"To Mr. Kapowski."

Emily clinked her glass against his, her lips pursed into a smile. "Mr. Kapowski." She took a sip, letting the bubbles pop on her tongue.

"You're still not feeling confident about the whole thing, are you?" Daniel said.

Emily shrugged, her eyes focused on the liquid in her glass. She swilled it and watched the trajectory of the bubble streams inside change, disrupted by the motion, before settling again. "I just don't have much faith in myself," she finally said, with a large sigh. "I've never really achieved anything before."

"What about your job in New York?"

"I mean nothing I've ever wanted."

Daniel wiggled his eyebrows. "What about me?"

Emily couldn't help but smirk. "I don't view you as an achievement as such…"

"You should," he interjected jovially. "A stoic guy like me. It's not like I'm the easiest guy to chat with in the whole world."

Emily laughed, then planted a long, sumptuous kiss on his lips.

"What was that for?" he said once she pulled away.

"A thank-you. For this." She nodded to the small picnic spread before them. "For being here."

Daniel seemed to hesitate then and Emily realized why: because being here wasn't something that Daniel would ever be able to fully commit to. Traveling was in his blood. At some point he'd have to set off.

But what about her? She hadn't made any fixed plans to stay in Sunset Harbor, either. She'd already been here six months—a long time to be away from New York, away from her home and her friends. And yet, with the sun setting in the distance, casting orange and pink rays into the sky, she couldn't think of anywhere else she'd rather be. In this exact moment, right now, everything was perfect. She felt like she was living in paradise. Perhaps she really could make Sunset Harbor her home. Perhaps Daniel would want to settle down with her. There was no way of knowing the future; she would just have to take each day as it came. At the very least she could stay here until her money ran dry. And if she put in enough hard work, made the B&B sustainable, then that day might not come for a very long time.

"What are you thinking about?" Daniel asked.

"The future, I guess," Emily replied.

"Ah," Daniel replied, looking down at his lap.

"Not a good topic of conversation?" Emily queried.

Daniel shrugged. "Not always. Isn't it better just to enjoy the moment?"

Emily wasn't sure how to take that statement. Was it evidence of his desire to leave this place? If the future wasn't a good topic of conversation, was that because he had visions of future heartbreak?

"I suppose," she said quietly. "But sometimes it's impossible not to think ahead. It's okay to make plans too, don't you think?" She was trying to gently nudge Daniel, to make him give up just a sliver of information, anything that might make her feel steadier within their relationship.

"Not really," he said. "I try really hard to keep my mind in the present. Don't worry about the future. Don't dwell on the past."

Emily didn't like the idea of him worrying about their future, and had to stop herself from demanding to know what exactly there was to worry about. Instead, she asked, "Is there a lot to dwell on?"

Daniel hadn't revealed too much about his past. She knew he had moved around a lot, that his parents divorced and his dad drank, that he credited her own father for giving him a future.

"Oh yeah," Daniel said. "A whole lot."

He fell silent again. Emily wanted him to give more but could tell he wasn't able to. She wondered if he knew how much she ached to be the person he opened up to.

But with Daniel it was all about patience. He would speak when he was ready, if he was ever ready.

And if that day ever did come, she hoped she'd still be around to listen.

CHAPTER FOUR

The next morning Emily woke early, determined not to miss the breakfast shift again. At seven sharp she heard the sound of the guest's bedroom door opening and closing softly, then the patter of Mr. Kapowski's footsteps as he descended the staircase. Emily stepped out from where she'd been loitering in the corridor and stood at the bottom of the steps looking up at him.

"Good morning, Mr. Kapowski," she said confidently, a pleasant smile on her face.

Mr. Kapowski startled.

"Oh. Good morning. You're awake."

"Yes," Emily said, maintaining her confident tone, though she felt anything but. "I wanted to apologize for yesterday, for not being available to make you breakfast. Did you sleep okay?" She noted the dark rings around his eyes.

Mr. Kapowski hesitated for a moment. He nervously shoved his hands into the pockets of his crumpled suit.

"Um...no, actually," he finally replied.

"Oh no," Emily said, concerned. "Not because of the bedroom, I hope?"

Mr. Kapowski seemed fidgety and awkward, rubbing his neck like he had more to say but didn't know how to.

"Actually," he finally managed, "the pillow was quite lumpy."

"I'm so sorry about that," Emily said, frustrated with herself for not having tested it.

"And um...the towels were scratchy."

"They are?" Emily said, perturbed. "Why don't you come and sit in the dining room," she said, fighting to keep the panic from her voice, "and let me know your concerns."

She guided him into the vast dining room and opened up the curtains, letting the pale morning light filter into the room, showing off her latest display of lilies from Raj, the smell of which permeated the room. The surface of the long mahogany banquet style table glistened. Emily loved this room; it was so opulent, so fancy and ornate. It had been the perfect room to showcase some of her father's antique crockery, and they were kept in a display case made of the same deep mahogany wood as the table.

"That's better," she said, her tone remaining bright and breezy. "Now, would you like to let me know about your room so we can fix it?"

Mr. Kapowski looked uncomfortable, as though he really didn't want to speak.

"It's nothing really. Just the pillow and towels. And also maybe the mattress was very firm and um…a bit on the thin side."

Emily nodded, acting like his words weren't striking a chord of anguish in her heart.

"But really, it's fine," Mr. Kapowski added. "I'm a light sleeper."

"Well, okay," Emily said, realizing that making him speak was a worse course of action than leaving him unsatisfied with his room. "Well, what can I get you for breakfast?"

"Eggs and bacon, if that's not too much trouble," Mr. Kapowski said. "Fried. And toast. With mushrooms. And tomatoes."

"No problem," Emily said, worrying she didn't have all the ingredients he'd listed.

Emily hurried into the kitchen, awakening Mogsy and Rain immediately. Both dogs began yapping for their breakfast, but she ignored their whines as she raced over to the fridge and checked what was inside. She was relieved to see that she had bacon, although there were no mushrooms or tomatoes. At least there was bread in the bread bin, a surplus Karen from the general store had dropped around the other day, and eggs she could source thanks to Lola and Lolly.

Regretting her choice of footwear, Emily rushed out the back door, across the dewy grass, and to the chicken coop. Lola and Lolly were strutting about their pen. They both tipped their heads to the side at the sound of her approaching footsteps, expecting her to supply them with fresh corn.

"Not yet, little chickadees," she said. "Mr. Kapowski comes first."

They pecked their frustration at her as Emily rushed over to the hen house where they laid their eggs.

"You've got to be kidding me," she muttered as she looked inside to discover nothing there. She turned her face down to the chickens, hands on hips. "Of all the days for you two not to lay eggs, you choose today!"

Then she remembered all the poached egg practice she'd undertaken yesterday. She must have used at least five! She threw her hands up in the air. *Why did Daniel make me worry about poaching eggs?* she thought with frustration.

Emily headed back inside, disappointed that she wouldn't be able to provide the breakfast Mr. Kapowski wanted today either, and began grilling the bacon. Whether it was due to her anxiety or her lack of experience, Emily seemed unable to perform even the most simple of tasks. She spilled coffee all over the counter, then left the bacon under the grill too long so that the edges were crisp and black. The new toaster—a replacement for the one that blew up and ruined the kitchen—seemed to have much more sensitive settings than the last one, and she managed to burn the toast as well.

When she looked at what she'd produced, the final breakfast on the plate, Emily was less than satisfied. She couldn't serve that mess of a meal. So she went to the utility room and scraped the whole thing into the dogs' bowls. At least with the dogs fed that was one thing ticked off her to-do list.

Back in the kitchen, Emily tried once again to create the meal that Mr. Kapowski had ordered. This time, it came together better. The bacon wasn't overdone. The toast wasn't burned. She just hoped he'd forgive her for the missing ingredients.

She glanced at her watch and saw it had been nearly thirty minutes, and her heart raced.

She rushed back into the room.

"Here we are, Mr. Kapowski," Emily said, reemerging into the dining room with the breakfast tray. "I'm so sorry for the wait."

She realized as she approached the table that Mr. Kapowski had fallen asleep. Unsure whether to be relieved or annoyed, Emily put the tray down and began to back silently out of the room.

Mr. Kapowski's head suddenly sprung up. "Ah," he said, glancing down at the tray. "Breakfast. Thank you."

"I'm afraid I don't have any eggs or tomatoes or mushrooms today," she said.

Mr. Kapowski looked disappointed.

Emily went out into the corridor and took some deep breaths. The morning had been incredibly labor intensive, considering the amount of money she was ultimately making for her effort. If she wanted to sustain the business, she was going to have to become a little more efficient. And she needed a contingency plan in case Lola and Lolly had another lay-less day.

Just then, he emerged from the dining room. It had been less than a minute since she'd delivered his food.

"Is everything okay?" Emily asked. "Do you need something?"

Once again, Mr. Kapowski seemed reticent to speak.

"Um…the food is a bit cold."

"Oh," Emily said, panicking. "Here, let me heat it up for you."

"Actually, it's okay," Mr. Kapowski said. "I need to be getting on really."

"Okay," Emily said, feeling deflated. "Do you have anything nice planned for the day?" She was trying to sound like a B&B host rather than a panicking girl, although she felt much more like the latter.

"Oh, no, I meant that I need to be getting home," Mr. Kapowski corrected.

"You mean you're checking out?" Emily asked, taken aback.

She felt a cold chill spread over her body.

"But I had you down for three nights."

Mr. Kapowski looked awkward.

"I, um, just need to get back. I'll pay in full, though."

He seemed in a hurry to leave and even when Emily suggested knocking off the price of the two breakfasts he hadn't eaten he insisted that he just pay the bill in full and leave immediately. Emily stood at the door and watched him drive away, feeling like an utter failure.

She didn't know how long she stood there, lamenting the disaster that had been her very first guest, but she became aware of the sound of her cell phone ringing from inside. Thanks to the terrible reception she received in the old house, the only place Emily could get a signal was by the front door. She had a special hall table just for her phone—a beautiful antique piece she'd recovered from one of the closed-off bedrooms in the B&B. She paced over to it now, bracing herself to see who it was.

There were not many good options. Her mom hadn't been in touch since that emotional late-night phone call they'd shared in which they discussed the truth about Charlotte's death and, more specifically, Emily's role—or lack of—in it. Amy also hadn't been in touch since her cavalier attempt to "rescue" Emily from her new life, though they had made peace since. Ben, Emily's ex, had called numerous times since she'd upped and left but Emily hadn't answered a single one of his calls and now the frequency of them seemed to be diminishing.

She braced herself as she peered down at the screen. The name blinking up at her was a surprise to see. It was Jayne, an old school friend from New York. She'd known Jayne since she was a very young girl, and over the years they'd developed the kind of friendship whereby months would lapse before they spoke, but the second they got together it was as if no time had passed at all. Jayne had probably heard from Amy, or somewhere on the grapevine, about Emily's new life and was calling to probe her about the sudden and abrupt change she had made.

Emily answered the call.

"Em?" Jayne said, her voice bumpy and her breath ragged. "I just bumped into Amy during my jog. She said you'd *left* New York!"

Emily blinked, her mind now unaccustomed to the fast-paced style of talking all her New York friends shared. The idea of jogging while having a phone conversation was alien to Emily now.

"Yeah, it was a little while ago now actually," she said.

"How long ago are we talking?" Jayne asked, the sound of her pummeling footsteps audible over the line.

Emily's voice was small and apologetic. "Um, well, about six months."

"Yikes, I need to call you more often!" Jayne panted.

Emily could hear the background traffic, the honking of car horns, the thud of Jayne's sneakers as she pounded along a sidewalk. It evoked a very familiar image inside Emily's mind. She had been that person just a few months ago, always busy, never resting, cell phone latched to her ear.

"So what's the gossip?" Jayne said. "Tell me everything. I'm guessing Ben is out of the picture?"

Jayne, like all of Emily's friends and family, had never liked Ben. They'd been able to see what Emily had been blind to for seven years—that he was so not right for her.

"Truly out of the picture," Emily replied.

"And is there anyone new in the picture?" Jayne asked.

"Maybe…" Emily said coyly. "But it's new and still a bit unsteady so I'd rather not jinx it by talking about it."

"But I want to know everything!" Jayne cried. "Oh, hold on. I'm getting another call."

Emily waited while the line went silent. A few moments later, the noises of a New York City morning filled her ears again as Jayne reconnected.

"Sorry, babe," she said, "I had to take that. Work stuff. So look, Amy said you have a B&B up there or something?"

"Uh-huh," Emily replied. She felt a little tense talking about the B&B, since Amy had been so vocal about it being a stupid idea, not to mention the whole switch in Emily's life being ill thought through.

"Have you got any rooms available at the moment?" Jayne asked.

Emily was taken aback. She hadn't expected such a question. "Yeah," she said, thinking of Mr. Kapowski's now abandoned room. "Why?"

"I want to come!" Jayne exclaimed. "It's Memorial Day weekend, after all. And I desperately need to get out of the city. Can I book it?"

Emily faltered. "You don't have to do that, you know. You can just come and stay as a visitor."

"No way," Jayne replied. "I want the full treatment. Fresh towels every morning. Bacon and eggs for breakfast. I want to see you in action."

Emily laughed. Of all the people she'd spoken to about her new business venture, Jayne was being the most supportive.

"Well, let me book you in officially then," Emily said. "How long will your stay be?"

"I dunno, a week?"

"Great," Emily said, a little ball of joy rolling in her gut. "And when will you be arriving?"

"Tomorrow morning," Jayne said. "Around ten."

The ball of joy grew larger still. "Okay, bear with me one moment while I log you in."

A little giddy with excitement, Emily placed her cell on hold and rushed over to the computer at the reception desk, where she logged into the room-booking program and entered Jayne's details. She felt proud of herself for having technically filled up the B&B every day since it had opened, even if it only had one room to fill, and had only opened two days ago…

She rushed back to her cell and picked it up. "Okay, you're all booked in for one week."

"Very good," Jayne said. "You sounded very professional."

"Thanks," Emily replied shyly. "I'm still coming to grips with it all. My last guest was a disaster."

"You can tell me all about it tomorrow," Jayne said. "I'd better go. I'm starting my tenth mile so I need to save my breath. See you tomorrow?"

"I can't wait," Emily replied.

The call ended and Emily smiled to herself. She hadn't realized just how much she missed her old friend until she'd spoken to her. Seeing Jayne tomorrow would be a wonderful antidote to the disaster that had been Mr. Kapowski.

CHAPTER FIVE

Exhausted from her long, disastrous morning, Emily found herself sinking into unhappiness. Everywhere she looked she saw problems and mistakes; a messily painted wall, a poorly affixed light, an ill-fitting piece of furniture. Before, she'd seen them as quirks, but now they bothered her.

She knew she needed some professional help and advice. She was in way over her head, thinking she could just run a B&B.

She decided to call Cynthia, the bookstore owner who had once managed a B&B in her youth, to ask for advice.

"Emily," Cynthia said when she picked up the call. "How are you, my dear?"

"Awful," Emily said. "I'm having the worst day."

"But it's only seven thirty!" Cynthia cried. "How bad can it be really?"

"Really, really bad," Emily replied. "My first guest just left. I missed serving him breakfast on the first day, then on the second day I didn't have enough ingredients and he said the food was cold. He didn't like the pillows or the towels. I don't know what to do. Can you help?"

"I'll be right over," Cynthia said, sounding thrilled at the prospect of imparting some wisdom.

Emily went outside to wait for Cynthia and sat on the porch, hoping the sunshine might cheer her up, or, at the very least, the dose of vitamin D would. Her head felt so heavy she let it drop into her hands.

When she heard the sound of crunching gravel, she looked up to see Cynthia cycling toward her.

Cynthia's rusty bike was a common and somewhat unforgettable sight around Sunset Harbor, mainly because the woman sitting atop it had frizzy dyed orange hair and wore bright and very uncoordinated outfits. To make things even more bizarre, Cynthia had recently affixed a wicker basket to the front of her bike in which she transported Storm, one of Mogsy's puppies that she'd adopted. In many ways, Cynthia Jones was her very own tourist attraction.

Emily was glad to see her, though Cynthia's large red polka-dotted summer hat hurt her weary eyes somewhat. She waved at her friend and waited for the woman to reach her.

They went inside and Cynthia wasted no time. As they ascended the stairs, Cynthia fired questions at Emily, about water pressure, about whether she was serving organic food and who her supplier was. By the time they reached the guest bedroom, Emily's head was spinning.

She took Cynthia inside. The room, as far as Emily was concerned, was beautiful. There was a mezzanine area at one end where she'd put a comfy leather sofa so that guests could sit there and look out at the ocean view. The room was mainly white, but with blue accents, a sheepskin rug, and distressed pine furniture.

"This bed is too small," Cynthia said immediately. "Standard double? Are you crazy? You need something grand and opulent. Something luxurious, beyond anything they'd be able to afford themselves. You've made this room look like a bedroom showroom."

"I thought that was the point," Emily said meekly.

"Absolutely not!" Cynthia cried. "You need it to look like a palace!" She paced around, touching the crumpled bed covers. "Too scratchy," she said. "Your guests deserve to sleep in a bed that feels like silk against their skin." She paced over to the window. "These drapes are far too dark."

"Oh," Emily said. "Anything else?"

"How many rooms do you have?"

"Well, this is the main one that's ready. There are two more that just need some furnishings. Then there's a ton more that I haven't even managed to clear yet. And the whole third floor could be converted too."

Cynthia nodded and tapped her chin. She seemed to be having some ideas, perhaps, Emily wondered, some grand plans for the B&B that would be impossible for her to achieve.

"Show me the dining room," Cynthia commanded.

"Um…okay…"

They went downstairs and with every step Emily's dread intensified. She was beginning to regret the decision of asking Cynthia for help. Where Mr. Kapowski had dented her fragile ego, Cynthia was shattering it to pieces with a sledgehammer.

"No, no, no, no, no," Cynthia said, walking around the dining room.

"I thought you loved this room," Emily said, perturbed. Cynthia had certainly enjoyed the five-course meal and cocktails— made and paid for by Emily, no less—the last time she'd been here.

"I do. For dinner parties!" Cynthia exclaimed. "But you need to make this a B&B dining room now, with small tables so the guests can eat alone. You can't put them all on one big table like this!"

"I thought it would foster a sense of community," Emily stammered defensively. "I was trying to do something different."

"Darling," Cynthia said, "don't even go there. Not now. Maybe ten years down the line when you're an established business with money to spare, then you can start experimenting. But now you have no choice but to make this the way your guests are expecting. You understand?"

Emily nodded glumly. She didn't know if there was even going to be a ten years down the line. She'd only ever been thinking in the short term with the B&B and now it sounded like Cynthia wanted her to really invest in this place, turn it into something long term and sustainable. It was starting to sound expensive, and expensive was not something Emily could afford. Still, she listened patiently as Cynthia continued her critique.

"Don't put lilies in here. It reminds people of funerals. And oh dear God, that will have to move." Cynthia was looking out the window at the chicken coop. "Everyone loves a free-range egg but they certainly don't love seeing the dirty little critters that produced them!"

By the time she left, Emily was feeling worse than ever. She went back to sitting on the porch, looking at the to-do list Cynthia had given her. Just then, Daniel arrived home and strolled up the gravel path toward her.

"Boy, am I happy to see you," Emily said, looking up at him. "My day has literally sucked from the moment I woke up."

Daniel sat beside her on the porch. "How come?"

Emily regaled him with the tale of Mr. Kapowski, of Lola and Lolly failing in the one thing they were supposed to do, of the pretty shoes she'd ruined scrabbling around in their chicken coop, of the burned bacon, of Mr. Kapowski leaving, and of Cynthia's criticisms.

"And take a breath," Daniel said with a smirk as soon as she was finished.

"Don't laugh at me." Emily pouted. "It's been a really trying day and I could do with your support."

Daniel chuckled. "One day you'll look back and see the funny side. Once this is in the past and you're running the most successful B&B in Maine, that is."

"I doubt that will happen," Emily said, giving in further to her darkening mood. She couldn't begin to imagine her B&B becoming a success. She wasn't even sure if she could keep it going in the short term. "The worst thing is I know they're both right," she added. "I'm not good enough at this. I need to get better. And I need to make all the changes that Cynthia suggested. The B&B she managed when she was younger was one of the best in Maine. If I don't take her advice I'd be an idiot."

"How much work needs to be done?" Daniel asked.

"A lot. Cynthia says I need to get the other two rooms up to standard pronto. They need to be in different color schemes and have different nightly prices, so that guests feel like they have some kind of choice, to make them feel in control. She said that the chances are people will go for the middle-priced room because they don't want to look like they're stingy to their significant other, but that there'll always be a certain type of person who goes for the cheapest no matter what, and another who always goes for the most expensive."

"Whoa," Daniel said. "I never realized there was so much to think about."

"Neither did I," Emily replied. "I went into this whole thing blind and naïve. But I want to make this work, I really do."

"So what do you need to change? How long will it take?"

"Pretty much everything," Emily said glumly. "And I need to get it done as soon as possible. It's going to eat into the rest of my savings. I've worked out that I'll only have enough left to keep this place running until the Fourth of July. So one month."

Immediately, she noted the change in Daniel's body language, an almost imperceptible shift away from her. She was well aware that she was putting a time limit on their romance, as well as her business, and it seemed as if Daniel was already distancing himself from her, if only by a few centimeters.

"So, what are you going to do?" he asked.

"I'm going to go for it," she said, decisively.

Daniel smiled and nodded. "Why do anything halfway?" he said.

He put his arm around her and Emily leaned into him, relieved that he had closed the distance between them once again. But that shift wasn't something she was going to forget easily.

She'd started a stopwatch on their relationship and it was ticking down.

CHAPTER SIX

"This chest of drawers would be perfect for the smaller room," Emily said, her fingers running along the top of the pine dresser as she looked over at Daniel.

Her heart quickened as she fell in love, as she always did, with the hidden gems in Rico's antique store. She could see Daniel getting excited, too, as he eyed it; it was an added plus that this also happened to be their favorite place to go on dates together.

Both enjoyed the thrill of discovering rare and exotic items for the B&B, but they also loved the endless source of entertainment the old, forgetful man provided. While Rico's short-term memory was less than reliable, his ability to recall the past was second to none, and he would often launch into unexpected anecdotes about the townsfolk, or history lessons about Sunset Harbor itself. There was also often the added bonus of Serena, who, despite being fifteen years her junior, was someone Emily now considered to be a good friend.

Emily then looked up and saw an exquisite gold-gilded vanity mirror.

"Oh, and this would work perfectly too."

She flitted around the shop, Daniel following her as she hopped from one wardrobe to the next. As she went, she jotted down the prices and numbers on the tags of the items she was interested in, so she could give the list to Rico at the end. She was making numerous purchases, after all, and it was best not to confuse the poor man.

"What about this?" Emily asked Daniel, looking at a large four-poster bed. "Cynthia said that the beds need to be bigger. That I need to make my guests feel like royalty."

Daniel walked across the store from where he'd been examining some stone birdbaths, and stopped beside her.

"Whoa. I mean, yeah, your guests will definitely feel like royalty sleeping in that thing. It's enormous. Do you definitely have the space?"

Emily pulled out a measuring tape and began jotting down the dimensions of the bed, then consulted the diagram in her pocket. She'd written down all the dimensions to ensure she only purchased furniture that would neatly fit within the rooms. The plan was to stick to renovating the two other main rooms initially, pouring all her spare cash into making them as perfect as possible, then to expand quite rapidly to twenty rooms—the ones that would cater to the cheaper end of the market—once the money from the first three came in.

"It would definitely fit in the bridal suite!" Emily beamed. The beautiful bed frame was making her excited; just the thought of owning it and putting it in one of the bedrooms was a thrill.

Daniel reached out and looked at the price tag. "Have you seen how expensive it is?"

Emily leaned over and read the tag. "It belonged to a fifteenth-century Norwegian aristocrat," she read. "Of course it's going to be pricey."

Daniel gave her a bemused look. "Why are you not that concerned? The Emily I know would be hyperventilating around about now."

"Ha. Ha," Emily said wryly, though she knew he was speaking the truth. She was one of life's eternal fretters, but this time something had shifted. Perhaps it was that ticking clock, that tolling bell, the sand sifting through the timer of their relationship. Something about the finality of it all made her throw caution to the wind. "Spend money to make money, right?" she said, boldly. "If I scrimp now, I'll pay for it later. The B&B will implode."

"That's a little dramatic," Daniel said, laughing. "But I do know what you mean. You have to put in the investment now, put in the groundwork."

Emily took a deep breath.

"Okay, good. Now you're on my side, I'm ready to do this."

The thought of spending all that money from her savings, of ending up balancing so precariously on the edge of bankruptcy, was not something Emily relished doing. She'd never been that sort of person, the impulsive type. She was usually careful and considered, measuring the pros and cons of every situation before committing— that is, until she'd dramatically left her job, apartment, and boyfriend in New York and run away to Maine. Maybe she was more impulsive than she realized. Or perhaps it was a trait that was creeping up on her as she aged. Was that how Cynthia had become so eccentric—with every year she aged she added another luminous color to her wardrobe, dyed her hair another bizarre shade? As much as she loved her dear friend, Emily shuddered at the thought of becoming her.

Forcing her mind to stop drawing comparisons between herself and the older woman, Emily refocused on the task at hand.

"I suppose I'm buying it," she said to Daniel, almost willing him silently to tell her no, to give her an excuse not to go through with it.

"Cool," was all he said.

Just then Rico came over. "Ellie." He beamed. "So lovely to see you." The elderly man always had trouble remembering Emily's name.

"Hi, Rico," Emily said. "Do you have many more four-poster beds like this one?" She remembered the hidden room that Rico had shown her, the place where he stowed all the larger and often more expensive items he couldn't easily move. It was filled with treasures galore, more so than even her father's sprawling mansion contained.

"Of course," Rico said, patting her arm with a wizened hand. "They're in the back. Do you know where to go?"

Emily nodded. Rico had shown her and Daniel the secret corridor room several days earlier.

"In that case, take a look," Rico said. "I trust you."

Emily smiled to herself, wondering how he trusted her if he couldn't even remember her name. Then she and Daniel went along the unlit, winding corridor and into the expansive back room. Just like the last time she'd been here, Emily was almost winded by the cold, and overwhelmed by the sheer size of the vast room. It was like stepping into a cavern or cave. She shivered and pulled her arms about herself. Daniel noticed her shivering and drew her closely into him. The warmth coming off him comforted Emily.

They went deeper inside the room, passing cupboards and sideboards, desks and wardrobes.

"Narnia, here I come," Emily joked, pulling open the door to a particularly ornate wooden wardrobe, before jotting down its price and number on her list of purchases.

Finally, they located the place where all the beds were stored.

"Here," Emily said, looking at a dark wood, antique four-poster bed frame. Each of the posts was made to look like the tree trunks from which they'd been carved. It was almost otherworldly. "This is exactly what I need. Just one more like this and the high-end rooms will feel pretty darn luxurious, don't you think?"

Daniel seemed particularly impressed with the bed. "This is amazingly well built. I mean you can tell that by how well it's stood the test of time, but also the finish, the way they used a varnish that suited the natural wood effect." He seemed enamored, though no sooner had he said the words than he immediately became distracted by another bed. "Emily, quick, look at this one!"

Emily laughed as he tugged her hand to show her another ornate bed frame. This one had a paler varnish, and it almost looked like it was from an Icelandic log cabin. Patterns had been carved into the headboard and posts. It was gorgeous, a sight to behold.

"I mean, that's a one in a million piece, Emily!" Daniel said enthusiastically. "Hand-carved. Awesome carpentry. You'd pretty much put the B&B on the map if you bought this!"

Emily felt a warmth spread inside of her. It was true. The beds she'd found in Rico's store were amazing and unique. She could see now what Cynthia had been trying to tell her, about treating her guests like royalty. *She'd* certainly feel like a princess sleeping in one of these.

"You know," Emily said, her fingers idling over the wood of one of the posts. "If we buy these beds, there is one stipulation."

"Oh?" Daniel said, his eyebrows drawing together.

Emily pursed her lips and raised an eyebrow. "We'd have to try each one out. For quality assurance purposes, of course."

"You mean... Oh!" Daniel caught on to what Emily was suggestively implying. He wiggled his eyebrows. The prospect of buying the beds suddenly seemed even more enticing. "Oh well, of course..." he murmured, reaching his arms around Emily and pulling her into an embrace. "You wouldn't be able to rest at night if you didn't know, firsthand, the experience your guests were paying for."

He kissed her neck seductively and Emily laughed.

"I'm going to give Rico my list," she said, drawing herself out of the embrace. "And part with all of my money."

Daniel whistled through his teeth. "He's going to be happy. You've probably made him a whole month's profit in one sale!"

"I'm not thinking about that," Emily said, pretending to cover her eyes with her hands to avoid looking at the price labels.

She left Daniel in the large room and found Rico.

"Evie," he said when she reemerged. "Did you find what you wanted?"

"I did," Emily said. "I'd like to buy three wardrobes, a dressing table, two desks, six bedside tables, one tall boy, two chests of drawers, three rugs, and three antique beds."

"Oh," Rico said, a little surprised as she handed him the list of items and prices. "That's quite a lot." He began to add them up slowly on his ancient till.

"I'm furnishing two more rooms in the B&B and redesigning another."

"Ah yes, you're the B&B girl," Rico said, nodding. "Your dad would be so proud of what you've achieved, you know."

Emily couldn't help but squirm. Even though she appreciated his kind words, it made her uncomfortable to think of her dad.

"Thank you," she said quietly.

"Now," Rico said in his wizened voice, "since you're such a valued customer and you're doing something that will benefit the whole town, I'll give you a discount." He tapped some buttons and a figure appeared on the dusty display screen.

Emily squinted, not sure if she was seeing it right. "Rico, that's a fifty percent discount." She couldn't tell if the elderly gentleman had mistakenly entered the smaller figure; the last thing she wanted was to accidentally rip him off.

"That's quite right. You get a special Sunset Harbor Memorial Weekend discount." He winked.

Emily stammered, handing over her card. She could hardly believe his generosity.

"Are you sure?"

Rico waved a hand to silence her. The sale went through and Emily stood there a little dazed.

"Thank you, Rico," she said, breathlessly, and planted a kiss on the old man's papery cheek. "I don't know how to thank you."

He smiled wide, and that smile said it all.

She felt like a giddy child as she rushed off back through the antique shop to find Daniel.

"Rico gave me a half-price discount!" she exclaimed when she reached him.

He looked stunned.

"That's amazing," Daniel replied.

"Come on," Emily said, impatient all of a sudden. "Let's get this stuff out of here and start fixing up the B&B."

Daniel laughed. "I've never seen someone so eager to end a date."

"I'm sorry," Emily said with a blush. "It's just there's so much to do and prepare for when Jayne gets here."

"Who's Jayne?" Daniel asked. "You didn't tell me you'd booked another guest." He seemed excited for her, if not a little surprised.

Emily laughed. "Oh, it's not like that. Jayne's my old best friend from New York."

Daniel seemed suddenly awkward. He'd felt judged by Amy when she'd visited and was more than a little reticent to meet any of Emily's other friends.

"Okay," he said in a half mumble.

"She's nice," Emily reassured him. "And she'll love you." She kissed him on the cheek.

"You can't know that for certain," Daniel said. "You never know—people rub each other the wrong way all the time. And it's not like I'm the friendliest guy in the world."

Emily slung her arms around his neck and nuzzled in. "I promise. She'll love you because I love you. That's how it works with best friends."

Emily realized, after she'd spoken, that she had said the "L" word. She'd told Daniel she loved him. It had just slipped out, but she didn't feel strange or anxious about it at all. In fact, saying it had felt like the most natural thing in the world. She noted, however, that Daniel did not say it back and wondered whether she'd crossed that line too soon.

The two of them stayed like that for a while, quietly embracing in the dark antique store, as Emily mulled over the meaning of Daniel's silence in her mind.

*

The sky was dimming as they unloaded the heavy new four-poster beds from the back of Daniel's truck and carried them up to the rooms. They spent the next few hours putting them together and arranging the rooms, neither commenting on the words that had passed between them back at Rico's store.

As the sky blackened, Emily began to feel like the house was becoming more like a real B&B, like she'd committed more fully to the idea. In many ways, she had reached the point of no return. Not just with the B&B, but with her feelings for Daniel. She loved him. She loved the B&B. And she had no doubt in her mind about either.

"I think we should stay at mine tonight," Daniel announced when the clock struck midnight.

"Sure," Emily said, a little taken aback. She had never stayed the night in Daniel's carriage house and wondered whether it was some kind of attempt on his behalf to show his commitment to her when he'd failed earlier to say those three little words.

They locked up the B&B and crossed the lawn to where Daniel's small carriage house stood in darkness. He opened the door and showed Emily inside.

Emily always felt so much younger whenever she went to Daniel's house. Something about his vast collection of records and books intimidated her. She scanned the shelves now, looking at all the academic texts Daniel owned. Psychology. Photography. He had books on many different subjects. And, much to Emily's amusement, these intimidating-looking academic texts were all sandwiched between pulpy crime novels.

"No way!" she exclaimed. "You read Agatha Christie?"

Daniel just shrugged. "Nothing wrong with an Agatha now and again. She's a great storyteller."

"But aren't her books for middle-aged women?"

"Why don't you read one and tell me?" he said cheekily.

Emily smacked him with a pillow. "How dare you. Thirty-five is hardly middle-aged!"

They laughed as Daniel wrestled Emily down onto the couch. He tickled her mercilessly, making her squeal and pummel his back with closed fists. Then they both fell, exhausted from the play-fight, into a tangle of limbs. Emily's giggles died down. She panted, catching her breath, her arms wrapped around Daniel, twining her fingers through his hair. Their silly moods faded away, becoming more serious.

Daniel pulled back so he could see her face. "You're beautiful, you know," he said. "I'm not sure whether I tell you that enough."

Emily could tell the subtext of what he was saying. He was referring to earlier, to his not having told her that he loved her too. He was trying to make up for it now by showering her with compliments. It wasn't really the same thing, but she was happy to hear it nonetheless.

"Thank you," she murmured. "You're not so bad yourself."

Daniel smirked, smiling the crooked smile that Emily loved so much.

"I'm so glad I met you," he went on. "My life now compared to where it was before you, it's almost incomprehensible. You've flipped everything on its head."

"In a good way, I hope," Emily said.

"In the best way," Daniel assured her.

Emily felt her cheeks turning rosy. As much as she enjoyed hearing Daniel speak these words, she was still shy, still a little bit unsure as to where she stood with him, and unsure of how close she should really let herself get considering how up in the air everything was with the B&B.

Daniel seemed to be struggling to say the next words. Emily watched him patiently, her gaze encouraging.

"If you went away, I don't know what I'd do," Daniel said. "Actually, I do. I'd drive to New York to be with you again." He took her hand. "What I'm saying is stay with me. Okay? Wherever that place may be, make it be with me."

Daniel's words touched Emily deeply. There was such sincerity to them, such tenderness. It wasn't love that he was communicating but something else, something similar or at least as significant. It was a desire to be with her no matter what happened with the B&B. He was banishing the ticking clock, saying he didn't care whether she didn't make it work by the Fourth of July, that he would be there with her still.

"I will," Emily said, gazing up at him adoringly. "We can stay together. No matter what."

Daniel leaned down and kissed Emily deeply. She felt her body grow warm in response to him, and the heat between them intensified. Then Daniel stood and extended a hand to her. She bit her lip and took his hand, following him in eager anticipation as he led her to the bedroom.

CHAPTER SEVEN

The date had been exactly what both Emily and Daniel needed. Sometimes they both became so weighed down by all the work at the B&B that it was easy to let such things slide. So it was no surprise when they both slept through their 8 a.m. alarm clocks. Emily in particular had some much needed sleep to catch up on.

When they did both finally wake—at what now felt like an absurdly late hour of 9 a.m.—they decided it would be best to enjoy some more time in bed, since they'd had such a good time between the sheets the night before.

They finally got up at around ten, but even then they enjoyed a long, lazy breakfast before finally admitting that they ought to head back to the main house to continue working on the new rooms.

"Hey, look," Daniel said as he closed the carriage house door and locked it behind them. "There's a car in the drive."

"Another guest?" Emily questioned.

They began to stroll together, hand in hand, up the gravel path. Emily glanced up at the house, where she could see a woman with glossy black hair standing on the porch, several bags beside her, ringing the bell over and over.

"I think you're right," Daniel said.

Emily gasped, suddenly realizing who it was standing there.

"Oh no, I forgot about Jayne!" she cried. She checked her watch. Eleven. Jayne had said she'd be arriving at ten. She hoped her poor friend hadn't been standing there a whole hour ringing the bell.

"Jayne!" she called, racing up the gravel path. "I'm so sorry! I'm here!"

Jayne spun at the sound of her name. "Em!" she cried, waving. When she noticed Daniel pacing toward them just a few steps behind, her eyebrows shot up, as if to say, "Who is this guy?"

Emily reached her and the two women embraced.

"Have you been standing here for an hour?" Emily asked, concerned.

"Oh, come off it, Emily. How well do you know me? Of course I didn't get here on time. I was about forty-five minutes late!"

"Still," Emily said, apologetically. "Fifteen minutes is quite a long time to stand on someone's porch.

Jayne stomped the decking with the heel of her boot. "Sturdy, solid porch. It did a good job."

Emily laughed. Just then, Daniel reached them.

"Jayne, this is Daniel," Emily said hurriedly, knowing she had no choice now but to introduce him.

Daniel courteously shook Jayne's hand, even while she eyed him like a piece of meat.

"Nice to meet you," he said. "Emily's told me all about you."

"She has?" Jayne said, her eyebrows rising up her forehead. "Because she's told me nothing about you. You're a well-kept secret, Daniel."

Emily couldn't help but blush. Jayne wasn't one for subtleties, or keeping her mouth closed when she really ought to. Emily just hoped that Daniel didn't search for meaning in her words and come up with conclusions that really weren't true.

"Want me to help carry your bag?" he asked.

"Yes, please," Jayne replied.

The second Daniel bent over to pick up her bags she craned her head to check out his backside. She caught Emily's eye and nodded her approval. Emily cringed.

"Let me take those," Emily said quickly, nudging Daniel out the way and grabbing the bags. "Wow, Jayne, these things are heavy! What did you pack?"

"Oh, you know," Jayne said. "Two outfits a day—daywear and nightwear—plus an extra something for a formal evening, just in case. Lingerie, of course. Facemasks and moisturizers, makeup bag and brushes, nail polish, hair straighteners, curling tongs—"

"Did you really need to bring straighteners *and* curlers?" Emily queried, lugging the bags over the threshold and into the corridor.

"—*and* crimping irons," Jayne added. "You never know what mood might strike." She grinned wickedly at Emily.

"Emily," Daniel said, "you seem to be struggling. Why don't you let me take those up to Jayne's room?"

"Thanks Daniel," Emily said, making sure she was strategically blocking Jayne's view of Daniel's butt as he bent over. "Why don't you put those in Room One please?"

The original guest room, Room One, was affectionately nicknamed Mr. Kapowski's room by Daniel and Emily, but right now Emily didn't feel like delving into that particular story. She knew she sounded weirdly rigid and formal asking him to put the bags in Room One, but at this point in time she didn't care; her sole focus was getting Daniel safely away from Jayne as quickly as possible, preferably without her ogling his ass as he climbed the stairs. The farthest room in the house seemed to be a good distance.

Emily turned to Jayne. "Let me give you the tour." She steered her friend into the living room.

"Oh my God!" Jayne squealed before the door had even closed behind them. "Is *that* the new man in your life? Tell me it isn't so! Really? How did you keep it so quiet? Why aren't you calling up everyone you've ever met, including your kindergarten teacher and the postman, to tell them you're dating a hot lumberjack?"

Jayne spoke incredibly quickly, and loudly, in a way that could give someone a headache after five minutes in her company.

"He's not a lumberjack," Emily whispered, feeling embarrassed. How had she forgotten how brash Jayne could be? What on earth made her think it was a good idea to invite her oldest friend to the B&B when doing so would mean her relationship was scrutinized? She didn't want her to scare Daniel off; she'd already done a pretty good job of that herself by blurting out that she loved him yesterday.

"But girlfriend," Jayne added, "he is seriously hot. You can see that, right? I mean I know your tastes have gone all wacky over the last few months but you can still see a hot guy when he's standing in front of you, right?"

"Yes," Emily whispered, rolling her eyes. "Please don't be weird with him. It's new. Really new."

"What do you mean weird?"

"Like don't say anything about babies or marriage. And don't mention Ben, or any of my exes. Or my mother. Please, God, don't say anything about how crazy my mother is."

Jayne laughed. "You really like this guy, don't you? I haven't seen you this anxious in a long time."

Emily squirmed. "Actually, yeah, I do. I think I'm in love."

"No. Freakin'. Way!" Jayne cried, the volume of her voice rising a thousand notches. "You're in love?"

Just then, Daniel entered the room. Emily froze and Jayne's eyes widened in shock. She pressed her lips together.

"Oops," she said loudly, looking from one mortified face to the other. "So Daniel," Jayne added, breaking through the wall of tension that had filled the room like a balloon, "tell me all about you."

Daniel looked from Emily back to Jayne and gulped. "Um, actually, I think I'll leave you ladies to it. The dogs need walking." He backed out of the room in a hurry.

Emily sighed, feeling herself deflate. It hurt her that Daniel was acting so awkwardly about the fact she was in love with him. She turned to Jayne.

"Can we get out of here for a bit? I could show you around Sunset Harbor. You've never been here and this is where I spent most of my summers as a kid so it would be cool to show you the sights."

"Babe, tell me what footwear I need and I'm totally on it. Are we talking hiking boots? Jogging sneakers?"

Trust Jayne to have brought every possible type of footwear with her.

"Actually, you know, I haven't been for a run since I left New York," Emily said. "It might be fun to do that. It's too beautiful a day to spend it in the car, and we'd certainly cover more ground than if we walked. We can take the ocean path."

"Sounds great," Jayne said. "I got so many calls yesterday after I finished speaking to you that I had to give up on the twelfth mile. I could do with a proper run."

Emily gulped. A proper run for her had never really gone further than five miles. Right now, after six months of laziness, she'd be happy just to hit two miles.

"I'll just get changed," she said.

She rushed upstairs, leaving the B&B at the mercy of Jayne. When she reached the bedroom, she found Daniel lying on the bed, staring at the ceiling.

"Are you okay?" she asked tentatively. "I thought you were taking the dogs for a walk."

"I just had to get out of that room," Daniel said.

"Oh," Emily replied, glumly. Was the thought of her loving him so repulsive he had to run away?

Daniel sat up, looking dazed. "I mean why does she have to talk so quickly? And loudly? And why does she have to say five words when one will do?"

Emily realized then that the reason Daniel had rushed away so quickly was not because of her but because of Jayne, because of her fast-paced New York way of talking. She laughed, releasing some of the tension that had built inside of her.

"You know I used to be just like her."

Daniel shook his head. "No way. I don't believe it."

"Yes way," Emily replied, insistent. "Just you wait. By day five you won't be able to tell us apart."

"Dear God," Daniel said, falling back against the mattress.

CHAPTER EIGHT

Jayne looked like a supermodel as she jogged beside the glittering waves, her hair flowing behind her, her limbs long and lithe. Unlike Emily, Jayne had hardly even broken a sweat. Everyone they passed checked her out, bowled over by her beauty, by seeing someone so stunningly attractive in their quiet, sleepy town.

"I don't even remember the last time I saw the ocean," Jayne said. "I mean other than during the drive over here. Sometimes New York makes you forget that there's anything other than roads and buildings out there."

"That's true," Emily replied, panting, finding it difficult to form even the shortest of sentences.

Raj was just putting some potted plants outside his shop when they passed.

"Hi, Emily!" he called.

She waved back, conserving her breath. Then she saw Parker Black in his wholesaler's van. Parker was a young man, only around twenty-three or twenty-four years old, with a mop of curly blond hair. He'd inherited the wholesalers at the age of just sixteen when his father passed away and had done a sterling job keeping the operation going. When Emily opened the B&B, she immediately knew she wanted Parker to be her wholesaler.

He honked his horn and waved.

"Get lost, ya creep!" Jayne shouted.

"No, no, he's not honking like that," Emily puffed, shaking her head. "That's Parker, my wholesaler. He's honking to say hello." She waved back.

"Oh," Jayne said. "Does everyone know everyone else here then?"

There was a hint of disdain in her voice. Emily recognized it because she'd shared the same views when she'd first arrived—of Sunset Harbor being a boring small town, filled with busybodies who knew each other's business.

"Pretty much," she panted, only she said it with a grin, because that fact was one of the best things about the town to her now, because she'd made so many friends since she'd gotten here and had changed her opinions of so many things it was almost unfathomable.

They reached the bridge that connected the island to the mainland.

"This is where my car broke down," Emily said, recalling the moment she'd become stranded on the bridge on her way into Sunset Harbor, just as a snowstorm had begun. It had been Birk who'd rescued her that night. Though it had been awful at the time, Emily now remembered that night fondly.

"Uh-huh," Jayne said, seemingly uninterested. Her enthusiasm for the ocean had already seemed to wane. "Oh my God," she said, suddenly brightening. "Did you watch the last season of *Singing Sensations*?"

"Nope," Emily said. "I don't have a TV anymore."

Jayne looked horrified. "Oh. Okay. Well, anyway, there was this one contestant who was literally the hottest human in the entire universe."

Emily listened patiently as Jayne spoke about things she now considered unimportant. Had she sounded so boring to other people once upon a time? Had she really cared about such trivial things? The only good thing about Jayne commanding the conversation was that Emily could focus on breathing, something that was becoming increasingly difficult the further they ran.

"How's life, though?" Emily asked as soon as there was a moment of silence. She wanted to know about actual stuff, not all this pointless TV gossip.

"It's all right," Jayne said. "I split up with Harry. You know that, right? Then I was seeing Brandon for a while. Still am. Kind of. We have a casual thing going on."

Emily nodded and focused on keeping one foot pounding in front of the other. "And work?" she asked when she realized Jayne had finished talking.

"A constant stream of never-ending crap," Jayne replied. "I'm so envious of you. I would love to have nothing to do all day."

Emily frowned. "I work," she said, though her shallow breath didn't allow her to embellish.

"Oh, come on," Jayne said. "It's hardly comparable, is it? Twelve-hour days in a New York office compared to loafing around in an oceanside B&B!"

"I work," Emily said more forcefully. "And I don't loaf."

Jayne looked over at her friend. "Are you red because you're mad at me or because of the jogging?"

"Both," Emily stammered.

Jayne drew to a halt. Emily stopped next to her. She bent over and gripped her knees, taking deep breaths.

"I didn't mean you didn't work," Jayne said, her tone sounding like one audible eye roll. "I just meant that there's clearly a slower

40

pace to life out here. I'm telling you I'm jealous of you. That's a good thing!"

Emily straightened up. Was that how she and her friends used to express themselves, through being jealous of one another? What was wrong with just supporting each other's ventures, rather than comparing themselves constantly to work out who was on top at any given moment?

"Maybe we should head back," Emily said.

"Because you're pissed at me?" Jayne said, and this time she did roll her eyes.

Emily shook her head, though that was at least fifty percent of the reason. "Because I'm exhausted."

Jayne didn't seem convinced. She checked her watch. "We've only done three miles, Em," she said. "Let's do two more, then we'll turn back."

Emily shook her head. "I can't do a ten-mile run, Jayne. It will kill me. I'm just happy to have gotten this far."

Jayne seemed put out that she was cutting their run short. "Fine. Let's head back. Go to a coffee shop to grab lunch?"

Emily thought of Joe's diner, one of the few places in town to eat during the day. "Sure," she said, uncomfortable at the thought of taking Jayne to a place she knew she'd hate, one that would only solidify her view of Sunset Harbor as a boring small town.

As they jogged back the way they'd come, Jayne talked the whole time: about the latest *Vogue* photo shoot, a new thriller she'd seen at the theater, her favorite designer's new summer collection...

Emily just let her talk. She realized that no response was required on her part anyway.

*

Later that evening, as the two women sat side by side in the living room sipping wine, Jayne seemed restless. They'd had waffles and coffee at Joe's diner—although Jayne had initially ordered a cortardo, much to the older man's confusion—then had bought a basket full of dark green leafy vegetables from Karen's general store to juice at home because there wasn't anywhere in town that sold juices. "You should open a juice bar!" Jayne had exclaimed. "You'd make a killing!" Emily hadn't bothered explaining that a town like Sunset Harbor had very little demand for such a place.

Then Emily had cooked Spanish omelets for dinner, using fresh eggs from Lola and Lolly, noting how Cynthia was completely right about people loving the idea of organic eggs but not about seeing the critters that produced them.

Jayne had changed twice throughout the day. Once out of her sportswear, then once again for dinner. She was now wearing a beautiful black dress, one that reminded Emily too much of the dress she'd been wearing the night she'd broken up with Ben. She herself was dressed casually in a pair of jeans and a sweater; it hadn't occurred to her to change for dinner.

"So what can I do while I'm here?" Jayne asked once they settled into the living room with their bottle of wine. "Where are the best clubs? Lounges? Concerts?"

Emily began to laugh. "There's a local pub but it closes at eight p.m."

Jayne's mouth fell open in shock. "Are you really telling me there's nothing to do at night here?"

"There's plenty to do," Emily replied. "Just not that kind of stuff. There's hiking and boating, that sort of thing."

"Hiking? Boating? Is this what you're into now?"

Emily tensed. Jayne was starting to sound like Amy.

"What does it matter what I'm into now?" she said defensively. "I'm happy. Doesn't that count for anything?"

Jayne reached out and touched her friend on the knee. "I'm not trying to be mean," she said. "It's just that you've changed so much I can't help but think it's because of your new man. I've known you your entire dating life and you have to admit that you do have a habit of changing for men—"

"That's not what this is!" Emily snapped. "I haven't changed for Daniel. I may have changed because of him but that's entirely different. And if anything has changed me the most it's this B&B. Can't you see how much more purpose I have in my life now that I have something to work toward?"

Jayne sat back. "I can," she admitted. "You seem good. Healthy. But from our perspective, you know, the friends that you abandoned, it looks a lot like you're just running away from your problems."

Emily pouted. She couldn't deny that that was indeed how this had all begun. She had fled the apartment she shared with Ben and endured the most horrendous few days in the decaying house while in the bitter grip of winter just so she didn't have to come face to face with any of her problems. But everything had changed since then. The house wasn't an escape for her anymore, it was her future. And she wanted nothing more in the world than to see it succeed.

"Why don't you come back to New York for a bit?" Jayne asked gently. "Spend some time in a city again. See how it feels now."

Emily crossed her arms. "Did my mother put you up to this?"

"No!" Jayne sighed. "I just want my friend back, Em. Is that so hard to understand?"

It wasn't. But what Jayne didn't seem to grasp was that her old friend was gone. The old Emily had transformed, morphed into this new woman sitting before her.

"Look," Emily said with a sigh. "I'm happy here. I have a purpose, a passion, at last. I'm determined to make this work."

"I can tell," Jayne replied. "But you've never run a B&B before. You don't have any experience and—"

"Oh, here we go," Emily interrupted. "I thought you coming here was to support me. But you're just doubting me like everyone has my whole life."

"Em," Jayne said, her tone persistent, "I worry about you. That's all. Do you really think this will work?"

Something about her words made Emily falter. She'd been able to express her doubts to Daniel only. To everyone else she was completely gung-ho, projecting the image of an unstoppable, determined woman.

"To be honest with you, no. I don't think I can make this work. The world is against me and I don't have the talent or the strength of conviction. But I'm not going down without a fight, Jayne. If there's a one percent chance I can make this work, I have to take it. I have to know I did absolutely everything in my power to succeed. That's the only way I'll be able to walk away with my head held high."

Jayne's eyebrows rose. "Whoa," she said. "I've never seen you like this about anything. Not even Ben and you were pretty determined to get him to marry you."

Emily just shrugged. "Like I said, I finally have a passion."

"I can tell," Jayne replied. She seemed momentarily defeated, or at least as though her fears had been somewhat quelled.

"Come on," Emily said. "We should be enjoying the evening, not arguing. Let's make cocktails. Sit on the porch and watch the sunset. What do you say?"

"You mean I don't need to go clubbing to have fun?" Jayne joked.

Emily laughed, relieved that the awkward conversation was finally over. She made up a pitcher of mojitos and the two women went to sit out on the porch. As the evening drew on, they talked about happier things, the pitcher of mojitos between them becoming emptier and emptier as their laughter became louder and louder.

Emily was bent over laughing hysterically at the anecdote Jayne had just told when she felt her friend's hand suddenly grip her. She looked up. Jayne's face had transformed and was suddenly pale.

"What?" Emily demanded. "What's wrong?"

Jayne pointed down the drive. As Emily followed where she was pointing she noticed the flashing lights illuminating the gravel of the driveway. Then her gaze finally settled on the police car and the two cops walking slowly toward her.

CHAPTER NINE

A swirl of nausea rose in Emily's throat. Her first thought was Daniel, that he'd gotten into a wreck during one of his drives up along the cliffsides. When she tried to set her drink down, she realized her hand was trembling.

But then she noticed that the cops weren't alone. There was someone walking along beside them who was very familiar to Emily. Trevor Mann.

Emily let out a huge groan. "It's just my neighbor," she told Jayne, speaking in one huge, relieved exhalation. "He's probably made a noise complaint."

Jayne raised an eyebrow. "Are you kidding? The cops will come out because some old guy doesn't like the sound of two cackling women?"

Emily laughed, feeling her anxiety fizz away. "We'll just smile sweetly, apologize, then finish our drinks inside."

Jayne shook her head. "Sunset Harbor is a weird place! Are you always expected to obey your neighbors' whims?"

"At the moment," Emily explained. "I don't have the energy to fight Trevor as well as try to keep the B&B afloat. He's too well connected. It's best just to appease him."

Emily watched as the three figures approached the house. But then she frowned when she noticed another car pull up, a car that was very familiar to her. It was the mayoral car. It drew to a halt and out hopped Mayor Hansen and Marcella.

"What's he doing here?" Emily said aloud as she watched the five figures congregate.

Together as a group they strolled up to the house. Trevor led them, looking proud and puffed up. The expressions of everyone else could be described only as ashamed.

"What's going on?" Emily asked, standing, her question directed right over Trevor's head and toward Mayor Hansen.

Of course, it made no difference to whom she'd addressed it; it was Trevor who answered her. "What's going on, Miss Mitchell, is that you're in breach of the town code signage regulations."

From behind, Jayne spat out her laughter. Emily turned and hushed her fiercely.

Trevor continued, his voice even more terse and pompous thanks to Jayne's mocking of him. "Your sign has to be taken down immediately or you'll be fined one hundred dollars per day that it remains in place."

The two police officers motioned forward as though to remove the sign.

"Now wait a second," Emily said, holding up her hands to stop them. "What are you talking about? Mayor Hansen?"

The mayor shrugged apologetically. "I'm afraid he's right, Emily. You need a special permit for the sign. Unless it comes down now, you'll be fined."

Marcella quickly pulled a piece of paper from her clipboard and thrust it toward Emily. "This is your cease-and-desist notification," she said. Then she added quickly, "And I also brought you an application form to apply for the sign."

"Thanks," Emily said dumbly, taking both pieces of paper. She skimmed the application form. "It says it takes a month for the application to be approved. You mean to say you're going to remove my sign for thirty days?"

"Or fine you three thousand dollars," Trevor added smugly. "You really should have done your homework before you decided to open up this place."

"Oh, that's what this is," Emily snapped at him. "You've spent the whole weekend researching ways to screw me over. This was the one thing you could get me on, wasn't it? You're a petty little man, Trevor. A sad, pathetic wretch."

"Whoo!" Jayne cried, laughing. "You tell him, Em!"

Trevor looked like he'd sucked a lemon. But he placed his hands on his hips, standing his ground. Emily looked to Mayor Hansen appealingly.

"You're not going to let him do this, are you?" she pleaded.

Rather than the mayor, it was Marcella who spoke. "He can't bend the law for you, Emily. I'm sorry, but rules are rules."

"Jeez!" Jayne cried from the porch. "You need to get that stick out your butt missy. Here, have a mojito." She thrust her glass toward Marcella, spilling the majority of its contents as she did so. Marcella looked disgusted and didn't even bother replying to Jayne.

Just then, Emily noticed the lights flick on in the carriage house. Daniel must have been disturbed by the commotion. The two policemen got to work removing the sign and Emily watched, her attention divided between them and Daniel's approaching figure.

"What the hell is this?" Daniel said as he reached them. His expression was thunderous.

"They're taking down my sign," Emily said in an exhalation. "I've broken some kind of violation."

"The town code signage regulation." Trevor Mann sneered.

Daniel shot him a chilling look, and then his attention focused, as Emily's had, on their hapless mayor. "Why are you letting him do this, Derek?" he demanded.

Mayor Hansen shuffled awkwardly in place.

"He can't bend the rules," Marcella said, repeating her words from earlier.

"I'm not asking you," Daniel snapped at her. "I'm asking him." He glowered again at Derek Hansen.

"Do you want to step back for me, sir?" one of the police officers said, approaching Daniel.

"Daniel," Emily warned. She could tell by his stance that he was coming across as threatening, and what with his previous criminal record, he really had to watch himself. Harassing the town mayor would not look good for him.

Daniel took a step back, but he was still fuming. "And you, you little toad," he said, pointing at Trevor. "You have some nerve. You're here for what, two months of the year, and you've decided to use them to tear someone else down? I hope you feel proud of yourself!"

"Actually, I've decided to move here full time," Trevor said, folding his arms. "I realized this dear little town needed more consistent vigilance to make sure such rules and regulations were being maintained."

Even the police seemed irritated by Trevor. But they did their duty nonetheless, keeping a protective distance between Trevor and Daniel.

Daniel's anger was starting to reach boiling point. Emily felt more than a little concerned that the police would get heavy-handed with him, which was the last thing she wanted to happen.

"Come on," she said to him, softly. "Let's just get inside." She put her hand on his back and guided him up the porch steps.

"I can't believe this," Daniel barked over his shoulder. "You're spineless, Derek. Do you know that?"

"Hush," Emily said. "Jayne," she added, addressing her friend, "let's continue this inside."

Jayne scooped up the mojito pitcher and glasses and followed Emily and Daniel inside, wobbling as she went.

As soon as they were inside, Emily turned to Daniel, needing his comfort now more than ever. Daniel already knew exactly what to do. He wrapped her up in his strong arms and held her. Emily pressed her face into his chest and squeezed her arms around his torso. She could hear his heart beating with anger, and could feel the heat coming off of him.

"I can't believe this," she murmured. "How am I going to get customers without a sign? No one will be able to find me."

Daniel pressed his mouth to the crown of her head with a hard, protective kiss. "It's only a month. You can make it."

"No, I can't," Emily stammered. "One month without any way of advertising the inn is a really long time."

"You'll just have to get creative. Advertise online. Make the directions really clear. It will be fine. Trust me."

"Maybe I should go," Jayne suddenly piped up. She was standing there looking awkward. "It looks like you have a lot on your plate here."

"No," Emily said, touching her friend's arm, suddenly aware that Jayne was being left out. "It's fine. I'm just annoyed because of my neighbor. I'll calm down in a bit and make another pitcher of mojitos."

Jayne gave her a small smile. "Honestly, Em, it's fine if you don't have time to hang out with me with all this sign drama going on. I can head back to New York."

Now it was Daniel's turn to look awkward.

"It's not 'drama,'" Emily said. "It's my business. My livelihood."

"Sure, sure," Jayne said, sounding more disinterested than ever. "I just mean I'm clearly in your way. And it's not like there's a bar or club I can escape to."

"You want to escape?" Emily said.

"I didn't mean it like that." Jayne sighed. "I mean that I feel like you need your space to do B&B things. I don't need to go anywhere. I could just hang out and watch TV but there isn't one of those so I'm not sure where to go to occupy myself while you're sorting this stuff out."

"Don't back-pedal now," Emily said. "I can read between the lines, not that your opinions were particularly hidden between them in the first place. This has nothing to do with you wanting to give me space. You're bored."

"That's not what I said," Jayne began to protest.

"But it's what you meant," Emily bit back.

Jayne stood there, floundering. Finally she said, "I'm going to head to bed. Don't worry about breakfast. I'll leave early."

She climbed up the stairs and Emily watched, her stomach feeling hollow, as she disappeared.

Daniel came up behind her and touched her shoulder lightly. Emily held onto the hand he'd placed there, needing it to ground her now more than ever.

"You okay?" he said gently in her ear.

She shook her head, still staring ahead at the staircase. "Not really," she murmured back.

"It's going to be okay," he added, as soft as ever, like the voice of reason calming the thunderstorm of thoughts and emotions running through her mind.

"Will it?" she whispered, so quiet as to be inaudible.

More than anything, Emily wanted to believe Daniel, but this time felt worse. She could feel it in her bones, that feeling like everything was ending, like it was all crashing on top of her. She'd poured everything she had into the B&B and she couldn't even make her oldest friend stay longer than one evening. With a heavy heart, Emily realized that she was on the brink of failure, that the dream she thought had come true was turning into a nightmare.

CHAPTER TEN

THREE WEEKS LATER

Emily was sitting in the kitchen with Mogsy and Rain when she heard the doorbell ring. The dogs' ears pricked up and Emily leaped to attention. Since her sign had been removed, she hadn't had a single customer. People didn't seem to trust a B&B without a sign and she could fully understand why. Her house looked just like every other house on the street. She wouldn't trust it either.

This was the first time anyone had rung her doorbell since the sign had been removed. She ran with excitement to the door and opened it. Two young men in nice crisp white shirts were standing on her doorstep. They grinned up at her.

"Hi," Emily said. "Are you looking for a room?"

The boys' pearly white grins grew larger. "Actually," one said in a Canadian accent, "we're here to talk to you about faith."

"Oh," Emily said. She noticed then the pamphlets in their hands. "I, um, well, I'm quite content with my … current belief system." She wanted to be polite but was utterly disappointed that the two boys weren't here for a room. She wanted them to leave as soon as possible. "I mean, I'm not looking to… switch to a different … higher being. Is that okay?"

The boys looked confused. They exchanged a glance. "May we leave some pamphlets?"

"Sure," Emily said. She took the illustrated, colorful slips of paper from their hands.

"May we come back again to talk to you another day?" the second boy added.

"Um… no." Emily didn't mean to be so abrupt, but she couldn't have people soliciting all the time, it would disrupt the business. "Sorry."

Even as she shut the door on the boys, their smiles didn't fade.

She felt bad about shutting them out and went upstairs to where Daniel was putting the finishing touches on the newest renovated room. It was looking great. If only she could get some guests to fill the place with.

"Who was at the door?" Daniel asked as he plumped the pillows.

"It was a religious call," Emily said glumly, wedging her shoulder against the door frame.

"Oh," Daniel said. "I thought it might be the photographer."

"He's coming tomorrow," Emily replied.

The B&B now had three high-end bedrooms and seven mid-range ones. Cynthia explained that each needed a photo for the website and a description of what it offered. Emily had been reticent about getting a website designed and paying for a photographer to take professional photographs when there was no money coming in, but she reminded herself that she had to put the effort in now if she wanted to be rewarded in the long run. Still, the Fourth of July was getting ever closer and there was no sign of the guests she'd need to fill the house and keep her business afloat.

"I guess we need to make a start on the other rooms now that these are done," Emily said.

"Third floor?" Daniel asked.

"Third floor," Emily said, nodding decisively.

She'd spent next to no time up on the third floor of the house. No one had, not even when her family had vacationed here. Emily had been avoiding it because she knew she would find it in the same state the house had been in when she first got here; decaying, cobwebbed, and crowded with memories.

"Want me to help?" Daniel asked.

"Of course," Emily said. Daniel's help was invaluable to her. She wasn't sure if she'd have even gotten this far if it weren't for him and his continued optimism, not to mention his ability to get her back up every time she fell. "Except I think there's going to be a lot of sorting to do. Through family stuff, you know?"

Daniel nodded. The process of decluttering the ground floor had been lengthy, made more so by Emily suddenly discovering a photograph or document, or an old family heirloom. That such treasures would be on the third floor was doubted by neither of them.

Daniel gave Emily a long, lingering kiss. "I'll see you tonight?" he asked.

"You bet," Emily replied.

The one good thing about having no guests was that Daniel and Emily had been able to vacation in each of the rooms for themselves. Somehow, amidst all the work, they'd managed to find the time for date nights and lazy mornings in bed. And in spite of Emily's dwindling bank balance, of the increasing feeling that time in the B&B was running out, their relationship seemed to be growing stronger every day.

Daniel left and Emily headed up to the third floor to begin the painstaking task of sorting the antiques from the mere dust gatherers, the sentimental from the hoarded.

The rooms at the top of the house must have originally been designed for staff. They were the perfect size for turning into the quaint, cozy, cheaper bedrooms that Cynthia demanded the B&B must have. Barry was due to come later in the week to start work on the piping systems for the en suite bathrooms, so it was essential that she got the rooms organized and cleared before then.

The first room Emily looked in was empty, except for a desk at the window and a chair. The shutters were broken, the wallpaper peeling, and an entire colony of spiders had made it their home. She shivered and shut the door again. The next room was in a similar state of abandonment. It had nothing within it expect for a ripped leather armchair facing the window with a footstool in front and a coffee table beside. She could imagine someone coming up here to read the paper. The yellow stain on the ceiling above the chair informed her that the newspaper reader had also clearly been a smoker.

In the third room, Emily discovered a box of her father's papers. Her father, she was realizing the more she explored the house, was an incredibly disorganized man. He seemed to have kept every scrap of paper, every letter, every document, and put it away somewhere in the house. And worse, the things that were actually valuable or precious in some way were locked within drawers. It had become a regular occurrence for Emily to attempt to open a drawer only to find it locked, to then discover that none of the numerous keys on the keychain she'd found in the safe in his study fit the lock. There was probably another safe somewhere, Emily thought, with another keychain, with a hundred more keys that opened nothing.

As she sifted through the box of decades-old bank statements, Emily thought about how she'd failed to pick up on this behavior of her father's. When he'd been around she hadn't noticed him being secretive. But the more she explored the house and sifted through his numerous belongings, the picture of the man that built up in her mind was someone who kept hold of everything. Though he'd sounded lucid in the note she found from him all those months ago, she wondered whether her father had had difficulties with his mental health, and that perhaps that was why he'd disappeared. She had found a prescription for antidepressants amongst his things, after all.

Emily shook the thoughts from her mind. It made her uncomfortable to think of her dad in this way, as though she were somehow dishonoring his memory. And anyway, thinking such things achieved nothing. There was no way of knowing what was going through his mind without the man himself here to explain. Ruminating on it would get her nowhere.

Emily put the box of old bank statements in the pile of items to be thrown away and then went to the fourth room.

This room contained more of her father's boxes. Some were neatly labeled—Roy's Books; Board Games; Newspapers 1997-1998—but others were just piled with random items. One box was filled with an assortment of items, from a bike chain to clothespins, to an ornamental candlestick and a bundle of computer cables. But then Emily saw something amongst the piles of junk that sparked her curiosity.

There were no lights in this room, but despite that, she noticed something across the room that was familiar to her. She stood now and walked over, craning her head to the side to see more clearly. As she drew up toward it she realized she was right; she was looking at another painting of the lighthouse.

She reached forward and picked up the framed painting, grunting from the effort, then rested it against the wall, the right way up, so she could get a better look. In this painting, the artist had painted it from the other side of the island, so that Sunset Harbor could be seen in the distance—a sliver of lights and rooftops. She went back over to where she'd found the painting and looked through each of the frames. Then, right at the back, she found another. The same lighthouse, only this one was painted at night, with the only source of light being the lighthouse itself.

Emily wondered who had had such affection for the little island that they had painted it in so many different incarnations. The signature looked like R. Wetherby. Or was it A. Westerly? She couldn't tell.

She put the two pictures with the other items she was keeping, the whole while wondering why her father had bought so many of those paintings. Was this more evidence of a disturbed mind, or was it just part of his hoarding behavior—why have one painting when you could have six? Or could it be something else? The artist must have been local. Perhaps it was a friend? Perhaps a lover?

Just then, Emily heard the doorbell ring downstairs. She checked her watch, surprised by how much time had passed. She was supposed to have made dinner!

53

She ran down the two flights of stairs and flung the door open to Daniel.

"Hi!" She beamed at him, kissing his cheek. "I have a confession to make."

He held up two bags of takeout. "You got so absorbed in sorting out the third floor you lost track of time?" he asked, laughing.

"You know me so well."

Emily stood back and let him inside. Daniel was still wearing his motorcycle leathers from having ridden to the next town over to collect their food, and he took them off as Emily dished out the dinner. Then they took their plates through to the living room and sat at the oval table beside the window.

"Do you know anyone called R. Wetherby?" Emily asked as she used her chopsticks to scoop noodles into her bowl. "Or A. Westerly?"

"Never heard of them," Daniel replied. "Should I have?"

Emily shrugged. "No. It's just that I've found more paintings of the lighthouse. I figured the artist must be local to have gone back and painted the same thing so many times. I thought you might know them, if they were local."

"No, sorry," Daniel said, frowning. "If anyone would know it would be Rico."

"That's true," Emily said. "I'll ask him next time I see him. Although I hope that's not for a long time, to be honest with you. I think I've given that man quite enough of my money."

Daniel laughed. "So how is it looking up there?"

"At the moment I've cleared all but three of the rooms completely. One room is stuff to sell. One is stuff to store. And one has all the antique decorations that we bought."

"That sounds very organized," Daniel said.

Just then, Emily's attention was distracted by a bright, flashing light from outside the window. At the same time, the dogs began yapping angrily.

"Did you see that?" Emily asked Daniel, leaping out of her seat and peering out at the black sky.

A moment later came the rumble of thunder.

"Summer storm," Daniel said. "My favorite. Why don't we sit on the porch and watch it?"

"What a romantic idea." Emily smiled.

They went outside, Mogsy and Rain following closely on their heels for comfort and settled at the porch table to finish of their meal. Every time the thunder rumbled, Mogsy would howl.

"You're not a wolf," Emily told her.

Rain was even more pathetic. He clambered up into Emily's lap and sat there shivering.

"You were born in a storm like this," she told the tiny puppy tenderly. "You were rescued by this beautiful damsel and a strong, brave man."

Daniel pretended to flex his arm muscles. Emily laughed.

Another bolt of lightning cracked against the sky and the rain started to fall more heavily. Rain the dog trembled even more.

"We should take these two inside," Emily said. "One of the rooms upstairs has a great view of the ocean. We could watch the storm from there."

They settled the dogs in their basket in the utility room, then went up to the third floor. Emily led Daniel into the room with the stained ceiling, the leather armchair, and the footstool. Daniel sat in the chair and pulled Emily into his lap. Together, they looked out the large, rain-splattered window as forks of lightning exploded across the sky.

"Makes me wish I still took photographs," Daniel said.

"Maybe you should," Emily replied.

"Nah. That's in the past," he said. "I don't think I even own a proper camera anymore. And anyway, I have more important things to think about now." He kissed her softly.

Another bright flash of lightning exploded over the sea. The rain that lashed the window pane became fiercer still.

"It's really coming down," Emily said, sitting up, suddenly worried. "You don't think this is going to turn into a storm like the one that tore down the outbuilding, do you?"

Daniel kissed her nose. "I'm pretty sure someone in town would have told me if there was a storm coming. You know what they're like."

Emily settled down again, resting against his chest. But she couldn't settle. She sat up again and turned to face Daniel with a worried expression.

"Do you hear that?" she asked, straining to hear over the rain.

"It's probably just the dogs scratching at the door," Daniel said.

"No, it's too steady, too rhythmical," Emily replied. She listened intently, trying to hear if she could catch the faint, rhythmic sound again. "It sounds like dripping."

She moved out of Daniel's arms and stood, then went out into the long, dark corridor. The noise became louder the second she left the room. It was coming from down the hall.

Daniel followed Emily as she paced through the gloom toward the noise. As she went, the noise became clearer until it was distinguishable.

"SHIT!" Emily cried as she threw open the door of the room in which she'd stored countless antiques. Water was cascading down the wall from the corner of the ceiling. "There's a leak!"

Daniel and Emily leapt to attention, rushing inside and moving items out of the room. Everything they touched was soaking. Emily tried not too think about how badly damaged everything was, but she knew in her bones that most of it was completely ruined. All that money. Wasted. And worse, there was a leak in the roof. She wouldn't be able to take a single booking if the house wasn't watertight.

Once everything was out of the room, Daniel wasted no time in getting into the attic to patch the leak. While he was up there, Emily went and checked the room directly beneath the one with the leak. There was now a horrible yellowish-brown stain in the ceiling and streaming down the corner of the new wallpaper. Emily felt her tears begin to well.

Daniel found her in the second-floor room, one of the high-end ones that she'd poured a lot of money into.

"I've patched it temporarily," he said as he entered. "So it will hold for the night. That will give you enough time to get a roofer out."

But his voice was smaller, quieter, as he became aware of Emily's devastation.

The storm had ruined their romantic evening, along with Emily's hopes for the future.

CHAPTER ELEVEN

The next morning was the type of beautiful morning that always came after a storm. It was so serene it was as though the chaos and destruction of the night before had never happened. In fact, the only evidence that the storm had happened at all was the fifty-dollar-an-hour roofer up the ladder inspecting the damage it had caused.

"It's gonna be five thousand dollars for the patch job," the man said once he'd climbed back down to solid ground. "But that's not gonna hold long because the beams beneath are weak and some of them are rotten. So I recommend you get the whole roof replaced."

"Oh God," Emily muttered. "And how much will that be?"

"Fifty thousand for the entire roof. But then you'll have a thirty-year guarantee."

"A thirty-year guarantee," Emily muttered to herself. "Thank goodness for that." To the salesman she added, "Is there anything I can do? Any deal you could give me?"

He twisted his lips. "Well, you can always source the materials yourself, then just pay for the labor. It's the slate tiles that would be the biggest expense, you see. It's not easy to get those things. Then, of course, you could use a different type of material but then it wouldn't be in keeping with the style of the property."

"What other types of material?"

"We could do shingle or asphalt. They'd be much cheaper. Here." He passed her a pamphlet. "This is all the options and all the prices." He turned the pamphlet over. "That's my direct number. Just give me a call when you're ready for the work to be done."

Emily took the pamphlet glumly. "Thanks for your time," she mumbled. "I'll be in touch."

Emily showed him to his van. As he drove away, she noticed Trevor Mann in his garden watching her with a sinister smirk on his lips.

Emily went quickly back inside, not willing to deal with a single one of Trevor's questions right now. The second the door was shut she let out the tense breath she'd been holding. As her mask of professionalism slipped, Emily's feeling of dread and depression intensified.

Just then, someone knocked at the front door. Emily gritted her teeth. She was not in the mood for Trevor.

The knocking came again.

"Emily?" she heard Daniel call from the other side. "You in there?"

She turned and opened the door. "Sorry, I thought you were Trevor."

"I won't ask why," Daniel said, frowning. "Was that the roofer I just saw leaving?" He jerked his thumb over his shoulder.

"Uh-huh," Emily said, her bottom lip beginning to quiver.

"Not good news, I take it," Daniel said.

"Nope," was all Emily could manage. She could feel the hot tears welling in her eyes, threatening to spill over.

"Come and sit down," Daniel said, leading her inside to the couch.

Just three short weeks ago, she'd been so hopeful about the future, about the B&B. To think there'd been a time when her greatest concern was that her guest had left before breakfast! She'd give anything to have Mr. Kapowski back if it meant a bit of cash flow.

"So, what are we looking at?" Daniel asked gently, his hand still wrapped around Emily's.

"Five grand for the patch job. Fifty grand for the whole thing, roof beams and all."

Daniel whistled. "Wow. Okay. It's that bad?"

Emily pressed her lips together and nodded. It was a warm day but she felt as cold as ice.

"Why did this have to happen just after pouring all my money into that antique furniture?" she cried.

"Well," Daniel said, "because fate is cruel. And life would be too easy otherwise." His quip fell on deaf ears. Emily was too depressed to laugh. "We can handle this," he said. "What if we sold off the carriage house?"

"We couldn't do that," Emily refuted immediately. "That's your home."

"I'll move in with you."

Emily shook her head. Not because she didn't want to live with Daniel—she most certainly did—but because she wanted it to be under happier circumstances, out of choice rather than necessity.

"I'm touched," she told him. "Really I am. It would be a huge sacrifice on your part. But I have to refuse."

Daniel didn't press it further. "Well then, why don't I take a job on the side? I could use the money to pay for the repairs."

Emily was deeply touched by Daniel's suggestions, but she didn't want him sacrificing so much for her benefit. She needed him to keep living his life as he wanted to, not living it in ways she needed him to. It was a surefire way to build resentment and she didn't want to risk it, not while everything between them felt so perfect.

Though she was more worried about her business than ever, Emily turned Daniel down.

"We'll find another way," she told him, squeezing his hand.

But what that might be, Emily had no idea.

Just then, the doorbell rang.

"Okay, this time it's definitely Trevor," Emily said with a groan as she stood from the couch.

Emily went to the front door. But when she opened it, it was not Trevor whom she found standing on the doorstep.

It was her mother.

CHAPTER TWELVE

Emily stood face to face with her mother for the first time in close to a year. She blinked, startled, as though she were seeing a ghost. Despite the difficulties in their relationship, Emily loved her mom and was still pleased to see her. She smiled warmly.

"So it's true," her mom said, not bothering with any kind of greeting. "I had to hear it from one of the yokels that my daughter was here. You know I knew you'd left New York, but that you came here of all places!"

Emily felt herself deflate. Her mom was on the offensive. Emily had run off to the house belonging to her father, the man who had abandoned their family without a word. She should have guessed that her mom would be livid when she found out, that this surprise visit from her mom wasn't for pleasure.

"I… I'm sorry I didn't get around to telling you," Emily began, trying to be diplomatic.

"Didn't get around to telling me?" Her mom tutted with disbelief. "Tell me, Emily, when were you expecting to get around to it? Next year? The year after?"

"Mom…" Emily said with a large exhalation, keeping her voice level even though her insides felt like she was on a rollercoaster. "I can explain if you give me a chance."

"I'd love you to explain," her mom said sharply. "I'd love nothing more than for you to tell me what the hell you're doing here."

Emily could feel herself growing angrier and more frustrated. She stayed at the threshold of the door, keeping a barrier between the house and her mom.

From over her shoulder, Emily heard Daniel call, "Who is it?"

"Nothing," she called back. "I can handle it." But when she looked back at her mother, her expression was more furious than ever.

"It is not nothing," she spat. "It's her mother!"

She shouted the last part into the house. Emily squirmed.

"Who have you got in there?" her mom added, prying.

"It's none of your business, Mom," Emily said, her patience running out. "Look, I don't want to be rude or anything, but it's late and I want to go to bed. I'm sorry I haven't been in touch but I'll call you first thing tomorrow morning and explain everything, okay?"

"Oh no," her mom replied. "I'm not buying that. I want you to let me in. It's been almost a year since we last saw each other and you seem to have created a secret little life for yourself in this awful place your father loved so much. Next thing I know you'll be telling me he's living here too!"

Emily shook her head, hurt that her mom would be so brazen as to pick the scab off that particular wound.

"Funnily enough," Emily said, "Dad is still considered a missing person."

Her mom pursed her lips. "Are you going to let me in or not?"

Emily faltered, feeling like she had no choice. She didn't want to let her angry, chaotic mother into the warm, happy world she'd created. She didn't want Daniel tarnished in any way by meeting her. But it was her mother, it was late, and she couldn't leave her standing on the doorstep.

"Fine," she replied. "Come in. I suppose we've got some catching up to do."

Emily guided her mom into the living room. Daniel stood up immediately from the couch when they entered, smoothing his hands over the tops of his trousers awkwardly.

"Daniel," Emily said, "this is my mom."

"Patricia," her mom said by way of introduction, holding out her hand. "Who are you?"

"I'm... um..." Daniel looked appealingly to Emily, unsure what he was supposed to say.

"He's my boyfriend, Mom," Emily said finally. It was the first time she'd referred to him as such. She hoped it wouldn't freak him out. It certainly wasn't as big a deal as telling him she loved him and that hadn't sent him running for the hills. And anyway, if anything was going to scare him away it would be this meeting with her mom.

"Shall I leave?" Daniel said in a hushed voice to Emily.

"I can hear you," Patricia said shortly. "And no, you're not leaving. You're going to stay and tell me what the hell is happening in my daughter's life, since she isn't capable of telling me herself. Emily Jane, fetch us some gin and tonics, won't you?"

Emily hesitated, unwilling to leave Daniel alone in a room with her psychologically fragile mom. But he gave her a reassuring look, one that seemed to say, "I can handle this."

She rushed off and made the gin, surprised to find that her hands were shaking. All this time she thought Sunset Harbor was changing her, but here she was, still trembling like a child just because of her sharp-tongued mother. She tried not to berate herself too much as she carried the tray of drinks back into the living room; her mom was probably going to do enough berating for the both of them.

"So you have dogs now, do you?" her mom said as soon as Emily returned.

From the door, she caught Daniel's eye. He mouthed *sorry*.

Emily placed the tray on the table. "Yes," she said, trying to sound breezy. "Two. Mogsy was a pregnant stray we rescued and Rain is the runt from her litter. Would you like to meet them?"

"Absolutely not," her mom replied, reaching for her drink. "You know I hate dogs. Filthy creatures."

Emily sat down beside Daniel and took the strongest of the gin and tonics before drinking it quickly. She was going to need some Dutch courage to get through the new few hours.

"So," her mom began, leaning forward, "what I've gleaned from Daniel is that you fancy yourself a businesswoman now. You've turned my house into a B&B."

Emily gulped. "Ta-da," she said, gesturing with her arms.

"You don't get many guests by the looks of things," her mom replied without missing a beat.

Emily could feel her insides clenching. The familiar desire to smack her mother welled up inside of her, but she fought it, just as she had done for all the years she'd known the awful woman.

"I gather from your silence," her mom added, "that it's not going well."

"Business is a little slow just now," Emily replied, trying to keep her voice steady. It seemed to have notched up in pitch. "I had to apply for a permit to put up a sign and just as soon as I've got that I've no doubt that it will pick up again soon."

Her mom just shrugged, looking as displeased as ever. She took a large swig of her gin. "You know this place is mine, not yours."

She said it so nonchalantly Emily was completely stunned.

"No, it's not," Emily finally managed to stammer. "Mom, you always hated this house. You would never even come with us on our vacations here. But now that it's fixed up, you want it?"

"None of that matters," Patricia said icily. "Your dad left it to me."

"You're wrong," Emily countered. "This house was in dad's family first. It was left to him. After you guys divorced, it was left to me, not you. He has papers here leaving it to me." She had found them in one of her father's safes and prayed that they had survived the most recent drenching the house had taken.

"Oh really?" her mom said, laughing. "Can I see these papers?"

"Yes," Emily said. "Once I relocate them."

Her mom raised an eyebrow. "You've lost the legal documents saying this house is yours?"

"Not lost," Emily said, floundering, "just misplaced. There's been a lot of reorganizing going on around here. But I know they're somewhere safe." She could feel the tears welling in her eyes. She didn't want to break down here, especially not in front of Daniel, but she was furious.

"Right," her mom said, standing. "I think I'll turn in for the night."

"Turn in?" Emily said. "You mean to say—"

"Well, I didn't drive eight hours from New York for one measly G&T, did I?" her mom replied boldly.

"But we're in the middle of renovating the rooms for the B&B! Everything is a mess!"

Her mom scoffed. "You're not putting me up in one of your silly B&B rooms. I'll be staying in the master room, thank you very much."

"You can't," Emily refuted. "That's my bedroom now."

Her mom eyed her coolly. "You've taken my room?"

"It wasn't yours!" Emily bit back. The anger was rising and rising inside of her. She was about to really lose her temper. "You got divorced, remember? That room was Dad's and he's not here anymore, so now it's mine. Why doesn't that make sense to you?"

She felt Daniel's hand on the top of her arm, holding her back as she had done to him several times before.

"We'll sleep in the carriage house," he said, diplomatically. "Let your mom have the master bedroom if she wants."

"Thank you, Daniel," her mom said smoothly. "I'm glad to see someone here respects their elders." And with that she clomped off upstairs, leaving Emily reeling beneath.

Emily grasped her mouth to stifle the wail that was bursting to get out. Luckily Daniel grabbed her before her knees hit the floor. He held her tightly in his arms as she gasped for air, hyperventilating.

"Look at me," he said, taking her face in his hands. "Emily, look at me."

She could hardly focus, her mind spinning, her breath coming in short, ragged gasps.

"My life…" she stammered. "It's collapsing."

"No," Daniel said sternly. "No, it's not. Emily. Stay with me. I'm not letting you have one of your blackouts again."

The words caught her off guard. "What?" she managed to ask. Her eyes were so blurred by her tears she couldn't even make out Daniel's features.

"The blackouts. When you get lost in the past and go silent and still. You had one at the Memorial Day Parade. And you had one before, during the storm. It scared me. I don't want you to disappear like that. I don't want you checking out of reality."

He knew. Daniel knew her secret.

"I have flashbacks," she stuttered. "Of the past. Of things I've blocked out."

Her face was still in his hands, his thumbs working overtime to wipe the tears from her cheeks as they fell.

"You've repressed your past and now it's coming back to you," he said gently.

Emily remembered the psychology textbooks he had on his shelf, next to the photography books and crime novels.

"Freud?" she said, managing a smile.

"Uh-huh," Daniel said gently. "And now with your mom here, it's triggering it more. But it's okay. Just stay with me."

Emily reached up and held her hands over his.

"I will," she said, her voice quiet now, the tears no longer falling. "I'll stay."

CHAPTER THIRTEEN

Emily wasn't sure if she managed to get even an hour's worth of sleep that night. Her mind was reeling, ticking overtime. She felt hyper, overvigilant, jumping at every noise.

As soon as her alarm went off at 6 a.m. she leapt out of bed. The last thing she wanted was her mom traipsing around the house unsupervised. If her mom was insisting on being here, at the very least Emily needed to keep an eye on her.

She dressed quickly and quietly, not wanting to wake Daniel. He stirred nonetheless.

"Are you going?" he asked sleepily.

"I should feed the dogs," she said, buttoning her blouse up. "And the chickens. And the dragon."

Daniel smirked. "Do you want me to come with you as backup?"

"You know what?" Emily said. "It would actually be really helpful if you kept out of the way. I don't like you seeing this part of my life."

"I can handle it," Daniel replied. "I have a crazy family too."

"I know. And you're probably going to avoid me meeting them for as long as possible."

"Fair point," he replied.

"Come on," Emily said, tucking him into bed. "Back to sleep with you." She kissed him tenderly.

Emily left the carriage house and trudged up the pathway, her arms wrapped tightly around her middle. Just knowing her mom was here seemed to taint everything. The wildflowers looked less colorful. The streak of silver ocean in the background made her feel nothing. Even the birdsong made her wince.

She reached the main house and went inside, padding along the corridor to the kitchen to make some coffee.

"OH jeez!" she exclaimed when she walked in to find her mom standing there. "How long have you been awake for?"

Her mom's hands were wrapped around a coffee mug. "A long time," she said. "Coffee?"

Emily eyed her suspiciously, but accepted the mug. She slumped down at the kitchen table, wracking her brain, trying to think of something to say.

"I don't want the house, Emily," her mom said suddenly.

Emily looked up from the tabletop.

"You don't?"

65

"No. I was hurt. Deeply hurt that you would come here of all places."

Emily swallowed hard.

"I know. But I didn't do it to hurt you."

"No," her mom said. "I'm sure you didn't. But it did hurt me. And I shouldn't have been surprised that you came here. I should have worked it out ages ago. You idolized your dad."

Emily held her mug tightly. She didn't know where this conversation was going, but she prayed it wouldn't be one of those ones where her mom berated her dad in one, long, angry stream of consciousness.

"He always left me to be the bad parent," her mom continued. "You don't remember that stuff though, do you? All you remember about him is his summer house. And the presents he'd get you. You don't remember the weeks he'd disappear off to Barcelona."

She was right. Emily had no memory of that at all. But she suspected that it wasn't something she'd blacked out, that rather it was something her mom had protected her from.

"And here was me thinking he only had eyes for Sunset Harbor," Emily joked, her voice cautious, not knowing how her mom would react.

To her surprise, her mom chuckled. Emily chanced looking at her. The fury she'd seen in her mother's eyes last night was gone.

"I worry you're going to turn out like him," Patricia said, sighing. "Disappearing. Running off."

"I wouldn't!" Emily protested.

"But you already did!" her mom argued back. "You ran off here without telling. I'm your mother. I need to know where you are, even if you don't want me to see you."

"I know." Emily looked back into her mug. "I'm sorry."

Patricia came and sat at the kitchen table opposite Emily. "I figure you've found out a lot of stuff you were protected from as a kid since you came here. Looking through your dad's stuff."

"Some," Emily said in a small voice. She sounded as much like a child as her mom made her feel. "I know he was on antidepressants."

"Okay," her mom said. "So you know you get it from both sides now."

Emily looked up and frowned. "You think I'm depressed?"

"I think you have a greater disposition toward mental health problems. Don't ignore them like your dad did." She reached out and took Emily's hands in hers.

Fighting her first instinct to flinch, Emily held hands with her mom. It felt incredibly uncomfortable to do so; she couldn't remember the last time they'd touched like this. She didn't want to talk about these things. She wanted to move on with her life. She was happy. At least she'd been happy before her mom turned up and ruined it all.

"I'm leaving today," her mom said. "Back to New York."

Emily's head snapped up to attention. "You are?"

Her mom nodded. "I was never planning on staying. I just needed to see you. And when it dawned on me where you might be I dug up a phone number of one of the locals, Karen, I think her name was. I just became more and more furious on the drive over and when I got here and saw you it all just exploded out of me."

This, Emily realized, was her mom's attempt at an apology. The likelihood of her actually saying sorry was slim, but in her own kind of way, she was explaining herself and, in doing so, apologizing for her behavior.

"You know how hard I find it to control my mood," her mom continued. "I'm trying some new meds at the moment. I'm always more wobbly when I'm changing the dose or type."

Emily shifted uncomfortably in her seat. Her mom had heaped years of responsibility on her shoulders and had always justified her behavior like this—either it was the meds, or it was because she hadn't taken them, or the dose had changed, or the type had changed. It was the same story every time and Emily just didn't have it in her to listen to it anymore.

"I need to get on," Emily said, standing. "The chickens need feeding and I have to walk the dogs."

Her mom nodded and let Emily's hands slide out from under hers.

"Is there anything I can do?" her mom asked as she walked away, "Before I leave?"

"Actually," Emily said, hitting on sudden inspiration, "wait one second." She rushed upstairs and rummaged in her bedroom drawer for the key that didn't seem to open anything. She found it, the iron cool beneath her palm, then ran back down to her mom. "Do you know where this key belongs?" She unfurled her hand, showing the key to her mom.

Patricia squinted. "Your dad had a lot of keys."

"I know," Emily said. "I've worked out where most of them go. But not this one."

Patricia looked closer. "It looks like one of the vault keys. They were long and silver like this."

"Vault?" Emily asked.

Her mom nodded. "Yes, in the wine cellar in the basement there are some vaults. Your dad used them for documents, some jewelry as well, I think."

Emily thought of the pearl necklace and letter she'd found in the safe in her father's study. Perhaps there would be more of the same in the vaults her mom was talking about.

Patricia looked up. "I'd try the wine cellar if you haven't already."

Emily didn't want to admit to her mother that she didn't even know of the existence of the wine cellar in the basement, that after over six months in the house she had only stepped foot down there once in order to get the boiler working.

"Thanks, Mom, I will."

Emily showed her mother to the door. At the threshold, her mom lingered for a moment.

"I'm proud of you, Emily Jane," she said finally.

"Thank you, Mom," Emily stammered.

She had never thought she'd hear her mom utter those words. To hear them now, when she'd been at her lowest, was a gift she would treasure for the rest of her life.

She shut the door and turned her back, her breath coming in sharp stabs. Seeing her mom had been an ordeal, but then she might have given Emily another clue to the mystery of her father. The key seemed to be burning a hole in her jeans pocket.

She wasted no time, rushing down into the dank basement. She followed the corridors, looking around for the wine cellar, and found it finally, right at the back, almost as hidden as the ballroom had been.

There were rows of dusty bottles of wine inside the cellar, but Emily was more interested in the small rusty vaults that sat beneath them. She sat on the cement floor and pulled the key from her pocket. She tried it in the lock of the first vault and to her utter delight it was a perfect fit.

The door to the vault creaked open and Emily looked inside. Just like in the upstairs safe, she saw something shimmering and something that looked like a piece of paper. She pulled at the paper, her heart beating wildly at the prospect that it might be another note from her father. But it was not. It was a sketch of a lighthouse.

"Not that damned lighthouse again," Emily muttered. She was getting a bit sick of seeing it.

She put the sketch back and reached in for the thing that was shimmering. Emily pulled her hand out of the vault and discovered sitting in her palm was a large diamond. She gasped, knowing immediately that it was real, that it was a piece of treasure her father had hidden. Had he done it for her? To keep it safely away from her mom's clutches during the divorce proceedings? Or was it more evidence of his befuddled mind, that he would put a diamond of clearly considerable worth in a vault, lock it up, and forget about it?

Emily held the diamond up to the light with one hand. The other clutched her mouth with disbelief. She knew what she was holding was valuable but she didn't even want to hazard a guess as to how much it would sell for.

She ran upstairs and hopped onto her computer, searching diamonds and local appraisers. Her heart skipped a beat as she read that the price could range between $3,000 and $27,000 per carat.

Excited, Emily wanted to call someone immediately to appraise the diamond, but it was too early for anyone to be available to call. She started researching, reading all about quality and cut, and how color affected the price. Then she read about diamond certification and leaped up.

She raced back down to the basement, still unfamiliar with the layout of the rooms and where the wine cellar was located. When she found it she rushed inside. The vault was sitting with the door still open. Emily reached inside and pulled out the sketch of the lighthouse. There on the back was the diamond's certification information.

Emily went back upstairs and started typing the information she had into her search engine. She hit enter and the figure that flashed before her eyes made her squeal with delight. The diamond was worth $10,000. Enough to partially fix the roof, although not completely replace it, with some left over to replace the items that had been ruined in the storm.

Emily sat back in her seat, stunned. She felt like her dad was communicating with her from wherever he was—Barcelona or heaven or somewhere else entirely. He had left this gift for her and hidden it so she could only find it when she needed it the most.

"Thank you," she whispered to the air.

CHAPTER FOURTEEN

On the white covers of Emily's bedspread, the diamond gleamed up at her, the light of her bedside lamp making it glitter. On the bed beside it lay the certificate of authentication, the lighthouse sketch on the other side visible through the paper.

Emily sat at the head of the bed, her phone wedged between her ear and shoulder, listening to the drone voice of a diamond seller on the other end. As she listened, her attention was transfixed on the diamond. She couldn't take her eyes off it. She rolled it in circles gently with a fingertip, only half listening to the telephone conversation.

Just then, Emily realized that the line had gone silent.

"Okay, thank you," she said hurriedly. "I'll be in touch."

She hung up the phone and sat back against the headboard, pondering the mystery of the diamond. Why would her father own such an item? As much as she wanted to believe that it was an investment he'd made to ensure there was something left for her to inherit when the time came, she also couldn't help but wonder if there was a connection between the diamond and the lighthouse picture on the certificate. It certainly meant that her father knew the artist personally as they must have been together when he or she sketched the picture. There were only two other explanations that she could come up with. The first was that the diamond and lighthouse paintings had nothing to do with her father at all, that they were relics from his own parents, who had owned the house first. The other was that the diamond and its certificate belonged to the artist originally and that her father had specifically bought the diamond in order to get the lighthouse sketch. The former seemed farfetched, the latter less plausible to her than the idea that the artist and her father were connected through a personal relationship.

Emily felt that same aching sensation in her stomach that she often felt when she attempted to decipher the riddle of her father. She hated speculating about him, though she did it often. But every possible scenario she came up with about his disappearance made her feel terrible, and this newest one—that he'd run off with his artist lover—made her feel worse than ever.

She tried to focus on the positives rather than the negatives. Finding the diamond was an amazing stroke of luck. Since its discovery, Emily had been calling as many diamond sellers and auctioneers in Maine as she could find, attempting to garner information about selling diamonds. It was another thing she felt woefully under-informed about; the last thing she wanted was to rush into a sale and get screwed over by someone who could smell that she was a novice from a mile away, leaving her with less money than the diamond was worth. She just hoped that Daniel was right, that the fact it was summer at the moment meant that there wouldn't be any more heavy downpours, because if the roof held for long enough, she'd be able to take a bit of time getting the sale of the diamond right before ordering for the patch job to be done.

She picked up the diamond, still too utterly shocked by the beauty and grandness of it to accept that it was really one of her possessions. In another world—one where she was rich and the B&B was a huge success—she wouldn't need to sell the beautiful diamond at all. She'd turn it into a pair of earrings and matching necklace. Or maybe she'd even keep it for her future wedding ring. It would be a way of feeling close to her father again, of having him walk her down the aisle on the day since he wouldn't be there in person. But this was not a perfect world. This was a world with broken slate roofing tiles and rotten beams that needed replacing.

Emily was jolted from her reverie by the sound of the phone ringing.

"This is Anne Maroney from Maroney & Stone," the voice on the other end explained when Emily answered.

Emily had been hoping it would be a booking and her hopes fell, dashed by the realization that it was just another diamond seller.

The woman on the other end continued. "I must say, the voicemail you left me was quite compelling! A lost diamond recovered from a vault after twenty years. The narrative really drew me in."

Emily felt herself brighten a little. Of all the people she'd spoken to so far, Anne Maroney was giving her the best vibes. She seemed kindly rather than just out for the money, and that really mattered to Emily. If she was going to part with something so precious of her father's, she wanted to do it right, and for it to be for a good person.

"I thought you may be able to book in a meeting with me," Anne said. "It could take place at my office in Maine, or I could come to you. I must confess, I had a look on your website and thought your B&B looked absolutely stunning. So my preference would be to come to you."

"Oh!" Emily said, delighted. "Well, that would be great if you don't mind the drive. I'd be very happy to meet you here."

"Wonderful!" Anne replied.

They booked a meeting to take place in several days' time, just after Emily's Fourth of July weekend cutoff. Anne's schedule wouldn't permit an earlier meeting, and though Emily knew it would be an agonizing wait for her, she had felt such warmth from Anne that she was certain this was the best course of action. Still, it was a risk to leave it so long. If there was another storm over the weekend that made the B&B leak again it would be a disaster for Emily, not just financially but emotionally too. She wasn't sure how many more setbacks she could take.

Emily took a small mahogany box—another one of her father's trinkets—and placed the diamond inside, then set it on the bedside table. Despite the relief of knowing that there would be money coming in from the sale of the diamond in the not too distant future, Emily also knew that the amount it fetched at sale would only be enough for the patch job on the roof. Replacing the rotten beams was going to cost significantly more, and acquiring enough money for that was going to be significantly harder. With every day that brought her closer to the Fourth of July, and every day that the B&B stood empty, Emily was starting to accept the very real and startling reality of leaving this all behind—the B&B, Sunset Harbor, the friends she had made... and Daniel.

So she had begun the task of mentally preparing. She stood up and pulled out one of the empty suitcases she'd stashed beneath the bed. She had already secretly packed one bag full with her stuff and was now moving onto the next. Her hope was that if she prepared for the worst then fate would intervene and throw something her way, some kind of lifeline, just like it had done with the diamond. Emily wasn't usually a superstitious person, but she felt that on this one thing she ought not tempt fate, and so was packing bags to throw it off.

As she folded some sweaters and placed them in the suitcase, she laughed to herself as she realized just how illogical that thought process really was. But her laughter quickly turned into tears at the thought of really leaving this place. She'd become attached to the house, the town, the people. Nowhere else felt like home to her now.

Emily couldn't help herself. She'd gone through so many trials and tribulations recently. She'd hardly even had time to process her mom's visit the other day and all the emotional dust it had stirred up. Unable to stop herself, Emily began to weep bitterly.

Just then, she heard Daniel climbing the steps. She quickly dammed her tears, then shoved the half-filled suitcase into the back of her wardrobe. Daniel would think she was crazy if she told him

72

she was packing to try and confuse fate and probably assume she was just running away.

She heard Daniel knocking at the door and leapt innocently to the end of the bed.

"Come in," she said, fighting to keep her voice steady.

Daniel entered through the bedroom door, his arms full of replacement rolls of wallpaper to cover the yellow water stain the leak had caused in Room Two.

"What's wrong?" he asked immediately.

Emily realized that her face was still tear-stained and her crying had probably made her eyes red and puffy. She wiped the tears off her cheeks quickly as Daniel propped the wallpaper against the wall and came and sat beside her. When he got there, he wrapped an arm around her shoulder.

"Sorry," Emily blubbered, feeling the tears well all over again at the sensation of human contact and affection.

"Don't be sorry," Daniel soothed her. "You can cry if you need to. Is this about your mom?"

Emily shook her head. "No. It's the B&B. I only have a few days left to get some paying guests or the whole thing is over."

Daniel took her wet cheeks in his hands. "You're very melodramatic, do you know that, Emily Mitchell?" he said. "Nothing's over. Do I have to remind you that you just discovered a ten-thousand-dollar diamond in your basement?"

She laughed in spite of herself. "Even so, I don't think there's anything melodramatic about the very real prospect of losing one's business."

"You won't lose the business," Daniel insisted. "It's going to be fine."

"But I haven't had a booking for weeks," Emily contested. "And the Fourth of July is just around the corner. The money from the diamond will only be enough fix the roof, not keep the place afloat. And what's the point of a fixed roof anyway if there aren't any guests to enjoy it?" She couldn't help but frown. "So I'm not sure how you can be so certain that it will be fine."

Daniel exhaled and squeezed her closer to him. "Because this is just life, Emily. It throws these things at you to keep it interesting. Sometimes you're down and out, sometimes you've got a beautiful girlfriend." He winked at her. "I just think something will come up. You wait and see."

Emily instantly put her fingers in her ears. "Don't tempt fate!" she shouted.

Daniel laughed and shook his head. He gently removed her fingers from her ears.

"I think you need a night out," he said. "You've been cooped up in this place on the phone to auctioneers all day."

Emily perked up immediately. "You want a date night?"

Daniel nodded. "It's well overdue, don't you think?"

Emily agreed that it was. "Do you have something in mind?"

But Daniel said nothing. Instead, his eyes twinkled mischievously as he stood and held his hand out to her.

"Maybe," he said. "Perhaps if you come with me you might find out."

"How very mysterious," Emily said, taking his hand.

Daniel led her down the stairs and out of the house. The sky was black and the moon barely a sliver. They strolled along the garden path hand in hand. With such little light, the foliage was dark and shadowy around them.

"Where are we going?" Emily asked, shivering, feeling a little spooked by the quiet and darkness.

"Just wait and see," Daniel said.

"You haven't restored another boat?" she asked suspiciously.

Daniel laughed. "Nope. But do keep guessing. It's funny."

Instead of walking down the sidewalk and out toward the town center, they went across the street and through the gap in the vegetation to the path—created by human feet—that was a shortcut down to the seafront.

"Intriguing," Emily said, trying to wrack her brain for any hint of what might be waiting for her. "Another rose garden?" she said, thinking of the time Daniel had shown her his secret flower garden.

"Nope. Try again."

Emily thought that there may be another picnic blanket and hamper in store, but when they reached the beach Emily saw that there was no picnic basket waiting for her. She wondered then if the date was going to be a romantic moonlit stroll beside the ocean. The ocean looked calm and so black she could hardly tell where the sea ended and sky began. Waves broke gently on the shore, creating a gentle backdrop to the sound of their pattering footsteps in the sand.

"Slow down!" Emily laughed as Daniel strode along the sand. "Moonlit strolls are supposed to be slow."

Daniel shook his head. "Still wrong. Guess again, Miss Mitchell."

Emily was stumped. She allowed Daniel to direct her westward along the beach. They never went this route, as the center of town was in an easterly direction. This was the part of the beach where the road running beside it sloped upward due to the cliffside. Daniel had ridden Emily on the back of his motorcycle along the cliffs a few exhilarating and slightly terrifying times in the past, but they had never walked along beneath them.

As they went now, Emily wondered why not. The cliffs were quite stunning from this angle and Emily smiled to herself as she thought about how even after several months in Sunset Harbor it still had secrets she'd yet to uncover. There were still places for her to explore. She just hoped she'd be able to stick around long enough to explore them all.

"Where *are* we going, Daniel?" Emily asked with an exasperated sigh.

"If you're all out of guesses then you're just going to have to be patient!" Daniel replied.

In the distance, Emily could see some lights twinkling. They seemed to be coming from the place where she knew there to be a yacht club. It was quite a fancy one on the water, probably with exclusive membership, which people on the zoning board like Trevor Mann and Mayor Hansen would frequent, and certainly not the sort of place for people like her and Daniel.

"You're not taking me to the yacht club, are you?" she asked with a frown.

Daniel just shrugged.

"Oh my God," Emily stammered. "You actually are, aren't you?"

She couldn't tell if Daniel was just teasing her by making it look like he was taking her to the fanciest place in Sunset Harbor. But they just kept getting closer and closer. The sound of music coming from the club grew louder as they approached.

"Okay, Daniel," Emily laughed when she saw the two black-suited doormen looking at them as they approached. "Joke's over."

Daniel grinned. "No joke, Emily."

Her mouth dropped open. "We're really going in?"

"Yup. They're having a free party tonight for locals. Everyone in town is coming."

"You should have said!" Emily said, thwacking him across the chest. "I'm so not dressed for this!"

"You look fine."

"Oh well, thanks," Emily said with glum sarcasm in her voice. "As long as I look 'fine.'"

Daniel stopped her, his hands on both of her shoulders. "I mean you look beautiful just the way you are."

Emily smiled shyly and accepted Daniel's gentle kiss against her lips. Then they went inside.

The yacht club overlooked the ocean, with huge floor to ceiling windows giving a panoramic view. The roof was steepled, with wooden eaves in the ceiling that gave it a feel almost like a church. Globe-shaped lights dangled from the ceiling on long wires, each one emitting a soft yellow glow that reminded Emily of hovering fireflies. The floor was wooden, varnished with the same mahogany finish as the floorboards in the B&B. All along one side was the bar. It had a marble countertop and was lit with warm yellow Yankee candles.

On one side of the club was a mezzanine floor; on the opposite a large brick chimney and fireplace. The decorations consisted of boat-related memorabilia, like small replica vessels, ships in bottles, and ancient-looking compasses.

As she walked in, Emily emitted a small gasp. It was all so gorgeous she couldn't help but feel instantly uncomfortable. The décor reminded her of the restaurants that Ben would take her to, fancy places where she had to dress up. She'd loved going to such places back when she lived in New York, but now she felt that she stuck out like a sore thumb, as though it was so obvious that she didn't belong in this kind of a place anymore.

She looked around at the guests in their fancy cocktail dresses and suits. She and Daniel were very underdressed for such an establishment, but Daniel didn't seem to care about that at all. He was in his usual plaid shirt and jeans, one eyebrow raised as he took in the splendor of the venue. The fact that he was so calm and confident made Emily relax a little. At least they were underdressed together.

"Want a beer?" Daniel asked her.

"Um, I don't think this is a beer kind of place," Emily said, looking around at all the people holding champagne flutes and wine glasses, or tumblers filled with amber liquid and ice cubes.

"Oh right," Daniel said, still not fazed. "I guess it's a brandy on the rocks kind of an evening. What do you want?"

Emily wasn't particularly in the mood to drink or dance *or* be merry. But as she looked around and spotted many of her Sunset Harbor friends amongst the crowd, she realized that she could use tonight as another opportunity to throw fate off the scent. She could treat it like a last hurrah, like a goodbye to everything she'd grown to love here. She was so close to the end anyway that really she had nothing to lose by letting her hair down for one evening.

"Wine," she said, finally. "White. Large."

"Sure thing," Daniel said, looking over at the bar where silver platters of canapés sat in a row. "Do you think those are free?" he added.

"I doubt it."

"I'll bring back as much as I can afford," he said.

Emily laughed and watched him move through the throng of people.

"Emily!" a voice called brightly, and Emily turned to see Karen from the general store approaching her. The two women had gotten off to a bad start when Emily first arrived in Sunset Harbor thanks to Emily's hostile and unfriendly attitude, but they were now on great terms. Karen was looking fabulous in a floor-length red silk dress. With her hair piled up on her head she looked ten years younger.

"Well, look at you!" Emily said, kissing her friend on the cheeks.

"Oh," Karen said, blushing and batting her hand as though to whisk away the compliment. "I haven't seen you for ages. How is everything going with the B&B?"

"Well," Emily began, not holding back, "Trevor got my sign removed so I haven't had any customers for weeks. And to be honest with you, if I don't fill the place up over the long weekend it's pretty much the end of the line."

"Oh," Karen said, her face falling. "I had no idea. You're not thinking of leaving Sunset Harbor, are you?"

"I wouldn't really have a choice," Emily replied. "There have been so many unforeseen expenses and I still have all those back taxes to sort out at some point."

Karen gave her head a little shake and wrinkled her nose. "I wouldn't worry about them. Mayor Hansen gave you an extension."

Like many of Emily's Sunset Harbor friends, Karen had supported her in the town meeting and had witnessed the mayor's generous offer to extend the deadline for Emily so she could get herself established first. Emily swallowed a lump in her throat, realizing then that the failure of her business would not just be her own; she would be letting down all the people who had supported her, including the mayor, who had flouted the rules on her behalf. He'd only done it because the B&B was going to be an asset to the town. But if it failed, she'd be letting the whole town down.

"He did," Emily said. "But Trevor's got his claws in with Marcella now, and she seems pretty good at getting the mayor to toe the line. They were all there when my sign was removed. I think Mayor Hansen's granted me more favors than I'm worth."

"I'm so sorry to hear that, Emily. I really am. Trevor is such a pest. The rest of us on the zoning board are beyond frustrated with him." Karen was on the zoning board too, though she never aligned with Trevor over his petty demands about how the town should look and, specifically, his obsession with Emily's B&B. "And now he's moving here full time!" Karen exclaimed dryly. "Well, I know I can speak on behalf of everyone else in Sunset Harbor when I say we all love having you here. You're part of the family now. And I'm not having Trevor Mann put your business in jeopardy. Let me speak to the other zoning board members. See if I can get a meeting about reinstating your sign."

It was a generous offer and Emily was touched. "You'd do that?"

"Of course," Karen exclaimed.

"And you think a meeting will help? I mean I've filled in all the necessary paperwork already and it said it could take up to thirty days for the application to be approved and the permit granted. It's been twenty-one already."

Karen patted Emily's arm then. "Up to thirty days providing no one's lodged a complaint or concern."

"Let me guess," Emily said through gritted teeth. "Trevor's lodged a complaint."

Karen nodded solemnly. "Look, leave this with me. I'll get a meeting to push the whole thing forward. Okay?"

Emily nodded, though the news that Trevor had delayed her getting a permit for the sign was making her less than hopeful. She might have to leave Sunset Harbor before a resolution could be found.

"In the meantime," Karen added, "if there's anything I can do to help, just ask."

"You could send me twenty more Mr. Kapowskis," Emily said sheepishly.

Karen patted her arm. "I'll send as many people your way as I can."

Emily thanked her, but she knew in her heart it would be too little too late now. Karen had sent her her first guest and she knew if there had been any more queries she would immediately have sent them her way. The reality was no one wanted to book a room at the B&B. And now the sign was going to be delayed too. Emily's heart grew leaden.

Just then Daniel reappeared, holding an entire silver platter of salmon bites.

"They *are* free." He grinned, handing her a glass of wine.

Emily took a sip of her wine, but she didn't feel much like wining and dining anymore.

"Did you bump into anyone interesting at the bar?" she asked. "I just saw Karen. She said Trevor's trying to stall the reinstatement of my sign."

"Oh," Daniel said. "That would explain why Mayor Hansen and Marcella were avoiding me at the bar." He reached out and rubbed Emily's shoulder. "I'm really sorry, Emily. Are you okay?"

She nodded, though in reality she was less than okay. "I think I need some fresh air."

"Sure," Daniel said. "There's a terrace that's worth checking out. You have to go up a spiral staircase to get to it." He pointed to the wrought iron staircase at the far side of the bar. "Do you want me to come with you?"

Emily shook her head. "I just want to have a little bit of time alone, if that's okay."

Daniel nodded and redirected his attention to the platter of canapés. "I have plenty to occupy myself with here anyway."

Emily smiled. "You have fun. I'll be back in a bit."

She left Daniel to munch on his snacks and wended her way through the crowd, waving at the friendly faces she saw, before climbing the staircase. It was stunning and she could imagine how amazing something similar would look in the B&B. She felt a pang of sadness at the thought that she might never get the chance to install one or have any guests enjoy it.

Up on the terrace, the ocean breeze whipped through her hair. Emily took a deep breath, the smell of salt familiar and comforting to her. The thought of returning to the smell of car fumes and pollution in New York was so unappealing to her now.

Emily walked over to the glass side of the terrace and leaned her arms on the rail. She looked out over at the ocean and the calm, black waves, feeling melancholy.

Just then she noticed an old man with white hair sitting at one of the tables alone, his sad face turned out toward the ocean in a similar manner to hers. Emily decided then that if she couldn't cheer herself up tonight, at the very least she could cheer up someone else. She went over to the man.

"Hi," she said. "I'm sorry to interrupt but I thought you might like some company."

The man's eyes twinkled as he looked up at her. He looked like he was in his early seventies. He was well dressed in a cream suit and he had a walking cane propped up beside his leg. "Well, that would be splendid. Please sit down, my dear. I'm Gus Havenshaw. Who are you?"

He had a privileged-sounding accent and Emily immediately suspected he'd gone to one of the East Coast's Ivy Leagues.

"My name's Emily," she said.

They shook hands and Emily sat down.

"What brings you to this establishment tonight, Emily?" Gus said. "Are you a Sunset Harbor local?"

"I am," Emily said, and she realized that that statement was more true now than it ever had been. She did feel like a local, like part of the family. "And you? Are you from around here?"

Gus nodded. "I grew up here. Went to school here. St. Matthew's, the Catholic school. Do you know it?"

"I do," Emily said, nodding. Cynthia's son, Jeremy, went to the exclusive private school, and Mayor Hansen had also attended in his youth.

"I like to come back every few years," Gus continued. "Sunset Harbor is the sort of place that gets under your skin. You can't be away from it for too long."

Emily smiled to herself, realizing just how much she agreed with the man. But she could see the sadness in Gus's eyes as he spoke. She wondered if his visits to Sunset Harbor were always alone, or whether he had any family to bring with him. It didn't seem right for him to be alone.

"So what brings you to the party?" Gus asked. "Are you a member of the club?"

Emily gestured to her jeans and shirt. "Do I look like a member?" she joked.

Gus let out a guffaw. "Well, no, I suppose not. But they do come in all shapes and sizes."

Emily raised an eyebrow. "Hardly. If tonight weren't free there's no way I'd be here. This place is for the elite only. Why, are you a member?"

Gus nodded. "You could call it that." His eyes twinkled then. "I'm one of the original investors. And I'm still one of the partners."

"Oh!" Emily said, suddenly embarrassed for her comment.

Gus just laughed. He seemed amused more than anything and Emily was glad she hadn't offended him.

"You know, you've been a good sport keeping an old man company," he said. "But I'm sure you'll want to get back to enjoying the party now. Don't feel like you have to sit here on my account. I'm just finishing my glass of port and then I'll be heading off."

"Actually," Emily said, "between you and me, Gus, I have a confession. I'm not really enjoying myself."

Gus looked shocked. "Now why is that? A young woman like yourself ought to be out on the dance floor until midnight. I certainly was at your age!"

Emily sighed then. Gus was more or less saying the same thing her New York friends thought, that by coming to this sleepy place she was making herself old before her time. Maybe she *should* be out on the dance floor every night.

"The thing is," Emily said, fiddling with her bracelet, "I'm having some problems with a dream of mine. Everyone's been telling me it was a stupid idea in the first place. For a second it looked like I was proving them all wrong, that the dream was coming true at first. But now I think it's about to fall apart."

Gus looked interested. "If you don't mind me asking, Miss Emily, what was the dream?"

Emily smiled then as an image of the B&B popped into her mind. She could visualize the sprawling porch with the large picnic-style table and benches, the yard-long corridor with its stunning polished floorboards and gorgeous cream carpet, the living room with the big fireplace and dark wooden bookshelves, the dining room that led to the amazing hidden ballroom with its Tiffany glass windows that sent shards of rainbow light dancing up the walls, and the kitchen with its original retro features. She had poured her heart and soul into restoring the house her father had loved and she realized now that she adored it more than she'd even thought.

"My dream," she said, smiling, "was to restore this beautiful old house that had fallen into disrepair and bring it back to life."

Gus looked interested. "I can tell by your eyes that this dream meant a lot to you. How far did you get to making it come true?"

"Pretty far," Emily admitted. "I got the house. Cleared it. Salvaged what I could. Restored what I could." She smiled again at the memories. "But then... well... it's a long story."

Gus chucked then. "I'm not going anywhere if you're not."

Emily found herself enjoying the old man's company so much she continued. It felt good to offload some of this with someone who was removed. She said, "There's been some misfortune."

"Some?"

"A lot."

He nodded. "Ah."

"Yeah," Emily said. "There are all these back taxes on the property to pay. Then there was a fire. And a storm. And a leak in the roof. So far I've poured every penny of my savings into the place and I still need more money to get everything sorted out."

Emily finished her story and was met by silence. She looked over at Gus and found that he was a very active listener. His eyes were wide, his mouth open with astonishment.

"You never told me," he finally said, "that you were turning the house into a B&B."

She shrugged.

"Did I forget that bit?" she said. "I guess it's not hugely relevant to the story."

He shook his head.

"You'll never believe what I have to tell you."

Emily was feeling more and more curious. She wondered what on earth it was he had to say.

"You came and sat with me because I looked glum, didn't you?" Gus began.

She nodded.

"Well, would you like to know the reason why I was so glum? I'm in awe at the amazing coincidence of it all. The reason why I was glum is because an event I was putting on had fallen through," he explained. "A St. Matthew's fifty-year anniversary reunion."

"Okay…" Emily said, wondering.

"Don't you see?" Gus exclaimed. "It was the hotel reservation that fell through! They'd double-booked us with a wedding party so naturally we were the ones that got canceled. I've been driving around all over the place looking for a B&B that could take at least some of us in but I couldn't find one anywhere. So I thought I'd stop off for a quick drink at my yacht club to give me the courage to call all my friends and tell them the party was off!"

Emily's eyes widened as it dawned on her what was happening. "You mean…"

Gus slapped his thigh and laughed loudly. "Yes, I do! Your dream has answered my wishes! I want to book your B&B!"

Emily was so shocked she didn't know what to say. Her throat was suddenly dry. She couldn't begin to formulate words so she just started laughing along with Gus.

The two of them sat there howling with laughter, tears streaming down their faces at the improbable coincidence, of the chance meeting that was an answer to each of their conundrums.

"I can't believe this is happening," Emily managed to say through her squeals of laughter.

Thank you, fate! she thought.

Gus's grin was infectious. She couldn't help but grin along with him. To the casual observer they must have looked like a strange pair of Cheshire cats.

"Well, Emily, we ought to get down to business then," Gus said. He coughed into his fist and rearranged his features, putting on a stern businesslike voice. "I'd like to book your establishment for twenty people."

Emily felt like she might faint any second. Gus's reunion party would max out the B&B! And just in the nick of time.

Despite the shock she was feeling, she managed to join in with the acting by putting on her best receptionist's voice. "No problem at all, Mr. Havenshaw. And how long will your party be staying for?"

"For four nights over the long weekend."

The news was like music to Emily's ears. Knowing the B&B would be full for the entire Fourth of July long weekend was beyond a joy, it was like a dream come true.

"That's wonderful," she said, keeping her voice as steady as possible. "I'll just take down your details."

Since Emily was nowhere near the software on the computer she needed to log his details, she just wrote them down on a crumpled napkin sitting on the table. She looked up at him, a little embarrassed, and broke character. "Math isn't my strong suit. I don't have the actual cost at hand. Would it be a problem if we sort that out when you arrive?" She chewed her lip in anticipation, suddenly wondering if she'd gotten way ahead of herself by celebrating.

Gus didn't seem concerned at all. "Our budget is two hundred fifty a night. At least that's what we were going to pay at the other place. So shall we just call it an even twenty thousand dollars?"

Emily's throat was so dry she could hardly swallow. Perhaps for a man like Gus, spending $20,000 on a single transaction was completely normal, but for Emily that was a phenomenal sum of money. She could hardly believe she'd gone from being flat out broke yesterday to suddenly having nearly $30,000 coming in from trade and diamonds! Daniel was right—life really did throw things at you for the fun of it.

She finally squeezed out, "Twenty thousand will be absolutely fine."

"Delightful!" Gus said, holding his hand out for her to shake. "I think that's a deal."

At that moment, Emily finally lost the power of speech. She shook Gus's hand vigorously, grinning wildly, making happy-sounding noises.

"Well, okay then," Gus said finally. He removed his hand from hers, though she clung on a little too long, as though unwilling to let go of the lifeline he'd thrown her. "I think this is the part where we exchange business cards."

Business cards! That had been one of the things on Cynthia's list of demands that Emily had not yet gotten around to doing.

"Oh, I don't have one on me," she confessed. "But here," she added, scrabbling inside her purse for the pen she had just put away. "Why don't I give you my cell number?"

"The personal touch," Gus said, looking impressed.

Emily smiled weakly, but attempted to play it off as intentional since he seemed to think so anyway. As she passed him the slip of paper with her number on it, the eternal worrier inside Emily wanted to ask him whether he was sure, whether he was really, truly sure, that he wanted to stay at her B&B, that he wanted to pay her $20,000 for the privilege. She had to hold her tongue to stop herself from blurting out that she was just pretending to be a host and that her B&B was actually make-believe, she was really just some silly girl from New York who'd started something that was now running away from her.

But she didn't say that at all. She kept calm.

"I look forward to welcoming you and your friends to the Inn at Sunset Harbor tomorrow evening," she managed to say, cordially.

"Thanks a bunch," Gus said. "You've saved my bacon."

And you've saved mine, Emily thought.

"I can't wait to call the others," Gus said, using his cane to propel himself up to standing.

"Do you need a hand?" Emily said, standing too to help him.

"No, thank you," Gus said. "I don't actually need a cane. It's just an accessory really. I think it gives me a sense of gravitas, don't you?"

"I guess so," Emily said. Gus seemed like quite the eccentric. She wondered whether the other St Matthew's alumni would be like him.

"I'll see you tomorrow!" Gus said.

Emily watched him walk across the terrace with a bounce in his step before descending down the spiral staircase and disappearing out of sight. The second he was gone, she fell back into her chair and let her mouth fall open. Had that really happened? It already felt like a dream.

Emily suddenly remembered that she'd left Daniel alone for far longer than she'd originally intended. She leaped up and rushed down the spiral staircase in search of him.

"There you are," he said as she rushed across the dance floor toward him. "I was worried that some handsome bachelor had whisked you off into the sunset."

"Almost," Emily said, grinning. "Except he was about seventy years old." She grabbed Daniel's hand. "You will not believe what just happened!"

Daniel frowned. "An *old* guy is whisking you off into the sunset?"

She shook her head but didn't have it in her to contain the secret anymore.

"Better! He's staying at my B&B over the long Fourth of July weekend. Him and nineteen of his old school friends!"

Daniel's eyes practically popped out of his head. "Are you kidding me?"

Emily shook her head, her excitement becoming impossible to contain.

"That's incredible," Daniel gasped. "Come here!" He swept her up into his arms and spun her around as she squealed. "I'm so happy for you. This is amazing, Emily. I knew it would all work out in the end."

"Okay, let me go now," Emily exclaimed. "We have a ton of work to do!"

Daniel set her down on her feet. They gave each other one last excited grin, then rushed back out of the yacht party and ran full pelt across the beach, kicking up sand in their haste to get home.

The dream was still alive, Emily thought as she ran. And for now, that was all that mattered.

CHAPTER FIFTEEN

Gus and his friends were due to arrive at 8 p.m. the next evening, meaning Emily had less than twenty-four hours to get the B&B ready. She knew the only way she was going get everything done in time was to call in every favor she could. So bright and early the next morning, incentivized by free food, Emily's Sunset Harbor friends filed in through the front door like a colony of worker bees.

The first arrival was George, Daniel's friend who had restored the Tiffany glass. He arrived dressed for a day of hard labor in paint-stained overalls. Birk came quickly on his heels, followed by Karen.

"I'm so thrilled everything worked out for you," Karen said, smiling jovially at Emily. "I couldn't believe that you managed to max the B&B out less than an hour after you'd been telling me you might have to close it down!"

"I know," Emily said. "It was a bit touch and go there for a while. But without my sign, things are still a bit up in the air."

Karen nodded. "About that," she said. "I've been on the phone to some of the other zoning board members. Trevor's complaint is going to delay the permit by at least another month."

"A month?" Emily cried, exasperated. This was the last thing she wanted to hear. She'd already had to hold on by her fingertips through three whole weeks without her sign; she wasn't sure she had the strength or willpower to hold on for another month. It wasn't like the world was full of rich old men like Gus waiting to book out her B&B.

"I know," Karen said, biting her lip. "It doesn't help that Derek has got Marcella as his aide now. She does everything by the book. I don't even think she likes Trevor, but she still makes sure everything is done perfectly." She squeezed Emily's arm. "It will be okay. I'm doing everything I can."

Emily nodded. But while she believed that Karen would do her best to help, she also knew that Trevor Mann was a formidable opponent. If he had Marcella on his side making sure everything was done to the letter it could be weeks before her permit was granted.

As Karen went inside, Emily decided she would have to put all of that out of her mind and focus on the present demands—sorting out the B&B, making sure everything was top-notch for Gus and his friends. She was determined to enjoy this weekend and make it perfect for everyone. At least then if everything fell apart, she would have the memory of this weekend to cherish.

Just then, Emily noticed Cynthia on her bicycle cycling up the driveway—the last helper to arrive. The older woman leapt off her bike and walked up the porch steps to where Emily was waiting.

"I thought early starts were a thing of the past," she grumbled. "It's been a good few years since I had to wake up at this time of the morning for a B&B."

Emily laughed and led her into the kitchen where the others had congregated. Daniel handed them all fresh coffee and bagels.

"Okay," Emily said, addressing the group. "We have until eight p.m. to get everything ready. That's only twelve hours! Daniel, can you oversee everything happening on the third floor? I have professional sanders coming to do the floorboards. George, you're replacing the window frames and glass in three of the top rooms. Karen and Birk, if you could please get all the furniture in place for the second-floor bedrooms, then once the floors are done we can get all the rugs, furniture, and bed frames up to the third floor." Then she turned to Cynthia. "I'm hoping you have some contacts from your days managing a B&B because I haven't managed to find a plumber willing to install sinks, showers, and toilets in twenty en suite bathrooms!"

"Sounds like you might need a whole army of plumbers," Cynthia replied. Then she beamed. "Leave it with me. I know just the men."

Tasks assigned, everyone disappeared to the upper floors of the B&B to get to work. Soon it was a hive of noise and activity—the grunts and moans of Karen and Birk as they wrestled wardrobes and dressing tables up the stairs, the constant background noise of the sanding machines as the professionals got down to business, the banging of hammers as George replaced some of the window frames, and the yammering of Cynthia on the phone as she called every contact she could to get the plumbing sorted.

Despite the chaos, Emily felt pumped and excited to see everything coming together so quickly. Barry and his army of plumbers arrived at 10 a.m. The window cleaner arrived a half hour later. By eleven there were more people tramping in and out of the house than Emily could count! It was so chaotic she hardly had time to wrap her head around the fact that by 8 p.m. she would have twenty functional rooms and en suites and every single one of them would be housing a guest!

At midday, Emily called for a break and all her friends congregated in the kitchen for sandwiches and chips, leaving the professionals to plow through with their work.

"How are the floors looking?" Emily asked Daniel as she made up a fresh batch of coffee.

"Pretty much done now," Daniel replied as he munched on his cheese sandwich. "I'm glad you got professionals in for that job. They're taking about half the time it took us to do the ballroom."

Emily smiled at the memory of the time she and Daniel had worked together fixing up the house. If she'd had more time, she would have preferred them to do it themselves. It was more romantic—and certainly cheaper!

Emily finished making the coffee and handed out mugs. But she didn't even have a chance to sit down for her own lunch because Raj Patel from the gardening shop arrived at that very moment with two huge bouquets of flowers in his arms.

"Oh my goodness," Emily cried out, rushing from the kitchen into the corridor. "Those are wonderful!" She took the gorgeous, bright flowers from Raj. "But how did you know I needed them? I haven't put an order in for weeks." With everything else she had to organize, it had completely slipped Emily's mind to order flowers.

"It's a small town," Raj said by way of an explanation. "Everyone knows the inn's going to be full this weekend. How long until they arrive?"

Emily consulted her watch and gulped. "Eight hours!"

Raj smiled. "You can do it," he said encouragingly. "Now, these are for the hallway," he explained, pointing to the summery bouquet that contained sunflowers and daffodils, "and these are for the dining room," he said of the more elegant bouquet, with white petunias, jasmines, and magnolias. "If anyone seems interested, let them know that I do weddings, christenings, funerals, the whole shebang. Here, I've got some business cards if you don't mind displaying them."

Emily certainly didn't mind. If Raj was going to supply her with free flowers the least she could do was send as much business his way as possible.

"Oh, I really need to order business cards at some point," she said, biting her lip, remembering her embarrassment at not having anything to give Gus the evening before. Not everyone would be as sympathetic to her disorganization. Plus, she didn't want to miss out on paying clients just because she hadn't gotten around to printing her number and address on a piece of shiny card! But there were too many other things that needed to be priorities—like making sure all the guests had a bed to sleep in and all the toilets flushed.

Just as Raj left, he passed Serena, who was flying into the corridor through the open front door, carrying several brown paper bags that seemed to be weighing her down.

"What are you doing here?" Emily gasped. She hadn't called on Serena's help because her young college friend lived a good two-hour drive away.

"Well, I went into that department store," Serena said excitedly to Emily. "And picked up all the things you wanted." She listed them on her fingers as she spoke. "Duvet covers, pillow sets in marine blue, racing horse green, crimson, and mustard yellow, and I even managed to get the matching throws."

Emily had asked Serena a long time ago on the off-chance that if she was ever passing this specific small independent store in the town where her college was located, to pick up the luxurious, bespoke bedding and drop them off next time she was driving down to Sunset Harbor. Although she had enough bedding for twenty guests, these were the specific kinds of sheets and bedspreads that Cynthia had suggested she use. But she hadn't expected the young woman to arrive quite so promptly, or to go so far out of her way just to help Emily out. She was a true friend, Emily realized, and was beyond grateful for her support and help.

"No wonder your bags are so heavy!" Emily exclaimed, looking through the bags with wonder at the beautiful colors and fabrics. "But I wasn't expecting you to go out of your way for me. You are amazing. Really."

"It's no problem," Serena said, rubbing the cricks from her shoulders carrying the heavy bags must have given her. She handed Emily the receipt. "The lady who worked there was thrilled, by the way. She said she hadn't had such a huge order in one go for years. I think she wants to come and stay at some point over the summer."

"Wow," Emily said, surprised. "Not only did you manage to buy all the bedding I need, you also potentially booked me a customer? I should send you out shopping for me all the time. Want to pick me up some new socks next time you're in town?"

Serena laughed. "Oh, before I forget," she said, searching through her bag and pulling out a small bundle of something secured with an elastic band. "Business cards!"

"Oh my gosh!" Emily cried as she took the bundle of cards from Serena. "You designed these?" They were a delicate eggshell blue and the font matched that of the inn's (currently absent) sign, as well as the website logo.

Serena shrugged. "It's no big deal. I just knocked them up using one of the college's computer programs and then my friend who works at a printing shop made a handful for me. I figured you would want some on the reception desk in case people wanted to take them."

"I do. They're amazing! Thank you." Emily hugged her friend, overwhelmed with gratitude and touched by the sweet gesture, even if Serena was trying to make it sound like no big deal.

"Right, so what needs doing next?" Serena asked, all businesslike.

"There's nothing more for you to do. Honestly. You've already done so much, getting the bedding and business cards. Just go in the kitchen, have a coffee, and eat some chips."

Just then, a man appeared at the front door. "I have a delivery for Miss Mitchell. Fresh salmon."

But just as Emily went to the door to sign for the delivery, the reception phone began to ring.

"I'll get it," Serena said brightly.

Emily rushed over to the door and signed for the delivery that had come from a local fishing company two towns over.

"Are the chips for anyone?" the salmon seller said with a cheeky grin.

Emily giggled, surprised. "I'll tell you what. If you put all the salmon away in the freezer for me then you can help yourself."

She grinned and the salmon man looked delighted as he stepped over the threshold in search of goodies. As he passed, Emily noticed Parker Black's van coming up the driveway and parking alongside the salmon supplier's truck. Parker had a suspicious look on his face as he went around the back of his own van and brought the boxes of organic fruits and vegetables Emily had ordered up the porch toward her.

"I hope you didn't just order salmon from someone other than me," he said with a warning tone. "I thought *I* was your wholesaler."

Emily took the box from him. "You're my fruit and veggie guy, not my freshly caught salmon guy."

"Why can't I be both?" Parker asked, sounding hurt.

Emily handed him over the cash for the delivery. "Well, you don't catch fresh salmon on a daily basis, do you? Because you know I can only have the best for my B&B. And if you're not catching it that day then I have no interest in it. But I'm very pleased with all these beautiful misshapen carrots and potatoes you sell me, so there's really no need to be jealous of the salmon guy!"

Emily thought they had been sharing a joke as they often did, but Parker looked glum as he hovered on her doorstep.

"Parker, are you okay?" Emily asked with concern.

The young man turned his blue eyes up to her. "I'm actually having some difficulties at the moment with cash flow."

"Oh. I didn't realize. I'm sorry." Emily knew all too well what it was like to struggle with money and the demoralizing effect it had on one's confidence. She felt embarrassed to have mocked him so mercilessly. "I promise I'll get salmon off you next time I order. How about that?"

Parker chewed on his lip. He looked suddenly very young, much younger than twenty-three. "Actually, I was wondering if you needed any help around the house."

"I need nothing but help around the house," Emily said. Behind her she could hear the footsteps of workmen running up and down the staircase while Daniel directed them where to go. "But I can only pay you in coffee."

"I meant something more permanent," Parker said.

Emily frowned. "Parker, are you asking for a job?"

Parker shoved his hands in his pockets. "I thought you might need a cook," he said, suddenly shy. "I actually spent a couple of years in culinary school. It was my dream to become a chef before everything happened with the wholesaler's."

Parker's usual arrogance had deserted him entirely and Emily was stunned by the turn of events. Not that long ago she had looked up to the younger man for running a successful business when she herself was floundering. Now suddenly the tables had turned. She was on the other side of the divide, on the cusp of success, which meant she now had the opportunity to help others.

"You know what," she said kindly, "I probably could do with some help at breakfast. I mean I'm not going to be able to juggle twenty breakfasts in one go, am I?"

Parker's face instantly lit up. "Really? Are you sure? You'll hire me?"

"If you say you can cook," she said, "then I'm willing to give you a chance."

Parker grinned his usual cheeky grin, transforming back into the same confident guy she'd come to know. "Emily, you're a lifesaver."

"I need you here six a.m. sharp," she said, raising a warning finger as if to say, *Don't mess this up.*

The young man smiled handsomely. "Sure thing, boss. See you tomorrow!"

Emily watched him stroll casually down the driveway and hop into his van, wondering if she'd made a terrible mistake. That she was now someone's employer all of a sudden was another thing to wrap her head around.

When she went back into the corridor she saw that Serena was still on the phone, politely dealing with what sounded like an overly persistent salesman. Emily grimaced but Serena kept smiling as brightly as ever. It dawned on Emily how amazing Serena was with people, with a natural charisma and a dazzling smile.

As soon as Serena hung up the phone, Emily said, "Hey, do you think you'd be able to help out at the B&B this weekend? Cover the reception desk when I'm busy, help greet the guests and show them to their rooms, serve breakfasts, that sort of thing? I'd pay you."

It seemed to Emily that if she was going to entrust Parker Black with any sort of responsibility, she ought to at least get someone she trusted more to oversee him when she couldn't. Plus, Serena was a student and always desperate for some extra cash.

"Really?" Serena said, grinning. "That would actually be awesome. But would I be able to stay over? I can't drive home every night."

Of the available rooms in the B&B, all of them were going to be taken up with guests. There were still some rooms on the second floor that hadn't been renovated yet, like her father's office, for example. She would just have to set a bed up for Serena in there.

"Yes, I can set up a room for you no problem," Emily replied.

"Okay then," Serena said. "I'm in."

Emily smiled. She was starting to collect a team. It amazed her how quickly everything had flipped on its head. She was really starting to enjoy this.

The day wore on, and Emily constantly kept a check on the time. It seemed to be going way faster than normal! The floors were done by 2 p.m., leaving the mammoth task of dusting and vacuuming. By 3.30 p.m. all the items of furniture had been maneuvered into the rooms on the third floor and everyone got straight to work making up all the beds. At 5 p.m. Emily called for another break. Everyone congregated in the kitchen for food and coffee, but Cynthia was nowhere to be found. Emily went into the living room and found her sitting at the piano, pressing down on some of the out-of-tune keys.

"I was just thinking that you should get this thing tuned," Cynthia said, "if Gus and his friends are St. Matthew's alumni. You know how much they love a good sing-a-long at St. Matthews."

Emily walked over to her father's old piano. It hadn't occurred to her to even check whether it worked or not; she'd simply had it cleaned and thought of it more as a decoration than an instrument.

"Do you know someone who might be able to do it today?" Emily asked. She looked at her watch. "Within three hours?"

"Of course!" Cynthia beamed brightly, snatching the cordless phone off the couch.

"Wait," Emily said, before Cynthia had a chance to punch in any numbers. "Will it be really expensive to get repaired? I don't know how much more money I can part with."

Cynthia gave Emily a look. "It'll cost no more than two hundred dollars. And you're about to make tens of thousands of dollars, my dear, so the least you can do is get this beautiful old relic back to playable standard. Jeremy has piano lessons with this lovely guy named Owen. I'm sure I'll be able to get him out this evening to tune it."

Just then, Emily heard the doorbell ring. So she relented, leaving Cynthia to sort out the piano issue, and went to answer the door. It was Jason, the firefighter she'd met the night her toaster had blown up.

"You're here for the pups," Emily said, feeling a tug of sadness inside her. Jason had agreed to look after Mogsy and Rain for the weekend since the house was going to be so crowded and loud. "I'll go and fetch them."

Mogsy must have sensed Emily's emotions because as soon as she entered the utility room, she immediately cast her sad eyes and began to whine, which set Rain off in turn.

"Don't make this harder than it already is," Emily said, hearing the hitch in her voice.

She clipped their leashes on and led them down to Jason's car, where baby Katy was sleeping contentedly in her car seat. Whether it was from the emotion Emily was already feeling at saying goodbye to the pups or something else, she felt a sudden overwhelming pang of longing. Baby Katy looked so perfect, so peaceful and innocent. Just like when Emily had seen the kindergarten kids in the parade, she felt the urge for children intensify.

Emily coaxed Rain into the trunk of the car with a dog chew, but Mogsy was a little more reticent and proved to be more stubborn. She dug her back legs in as Emily yanked on the leash.

"It won't be forever," she told the mama dog, crouching down and stroking her rough fur. "It's just for a little while. I'm not abandoning you, I promise."

Mogsy flopped her head heavily on Emily's knee, making Emily's heart ache even more.

"She'll be fine once she sees Thunder," Jason said gently.

Emily nodded sadly. Jason was right. They would have a great time hanging out with Mogsy's other puppy, but it was still heartbreaking to say goodbye. She'd grown far more attached to them than she'd intended over the last few weeks. They felt like her children, in a way, part of the odd little family she'd created with Daniel.

Emily finally managed to get Mogsy into the car, then watched as Jason revved the engine and waved goodbye. She kept watching the car until it had completely disappeared, the sound of Mogsy's whining audible the whole way up the drive.

Finally, her throat tight with emotion, she turned back to face the B&B. From here she could see through the open front door as people raced up and down. She could see Cynthia through the living room window on the phone to the pianist, persuading him to come and tune the piano. Several of the third-floor bedroom windows were open to air the rooms, and she could hear the sound of drilling and hammering coming from them. There was still so much to do before Gus and his friends arrived at eight.

Emily rushed inside to help finish up the last few bits. The last toilet was finished at 7.30 p.m. and Emily quickly ushered the army of plumbers out of the house. Then there was more sweeping and vacuuming to do, as well as scented candles to light in each of the rooms to dispel all the smells of varnish and glue. One by one, Emily's friends began to leave. Birk first, then Karen, then Cynthia and George, each wishing her good luck.

As the clock ticked ever closer to eight, finally it was just Emily, Daniel, and Serena. Emily suddenly realized that the special liquor delivery hadn't yet arrived. Gus had specifically asked for certain brands of wine and port to be in the living room on arrival. And while he was going to reimburse the cost of it all, it had been up to Emily to order it and pay for it up front. Parting with $1,000 was not something she relished doing.

Just then she heard wheels coming up the drive.

"Cutting it a bit close!" she cried as she rushed outside to the liquor van.

She handed a huge stack of dollar bills to the delivery guy as Daniel and Serena unloaded the boxes.

"Quick, guys, pour the wine," Emily commanded as she ran back inside to the living room.

As the last drop of wine splashed into the twentieth glass, the grandfather clock struck eight.

CHAPTER SIXTEEN

Emily stood on the porch steps, her stomach a knot of anticipation. She couldn't tell if it was excitement or apprehension, though it was probably both. She'd never felt so nervous.

The sun was just starting to set so Emily quickly lit the candles that led up the porch steps to the front door.

"Chill out," Serena said. "You need to relax."

Emily looked up at the young woman, looking every inch the hostess in a crisp blue shirt and black pencil skirt. She had her signature bright red lipstick on, which brought out her striking features and complemented her long, black hair.

Emily nodded. "I just really need this to go well."

"It will," Serena replied. "Don't worry."

Emily tried to relax, but Serena didn't know just how much was resting on this weekend. She couldn't help reeling things through her mind, panicking that she'd forgotten to do something. Her head was filled with everything from baked salmon to marine blue pillowcases, miniature shower gels to Denby crockery. She was certain everything had been done, that every box had been ticked, but that still didn't stop her from mulling every eventuality over in her mind.

Just then, a cream Rolls Royce turned into her drive and Emily tensed. "It's him. He's here."

Serena nudged her. "Smile, will you? You look like a funeral director!"

Emily transformed her expression into a welcoming smile, despite the sudden anguish she felt over her choice of an all-black ensemble.

The car halted and Gus got out. He looked almost identical to how he had when Emily had met him the night before, in a pair of cream chinos and matching cricket sweater, his cane at his side. Emily wondered whether the old man owned everything in cream and whether she should have decorated one of the bedrooms in cream specifically for him.

"There she is," Gus said with a smile as he climbed the porch up to Emily. "My angel from heaven." She took his hands and he bestowed a kiss on each of her cheeks. "And who is this divine creature?" he asked, looking at Serena and kissing her cheeks also.

"This is Serena," Emily said. "She'll be hosting this weekend alongside me."

Gus seemed utterly delighted and Emily was pleased that she'd made such a good choice in employing Serena for the long weekend.

"So the others are on their way," Gus said. "I must say we're all very excited. We hold a reunion as often as possible but this one is the most attended by far. I'm afraid we may keep you ladies up with all our singing. We St. Matthew-ites do love a good song. Ah, here they are now."

The familiar sensation of anguish returned to Emily as she watched several expensive-looking cars turn into the driveway and begin parking. Her heartbeat began drumming an even faster rhythm.

"Georgia!" Gus cried, greeting the first woman to reach the porch steps. "Come and meet Emily. Emily, this is Georgia Walters. Oh, and here's Hank! Hank Lloyd, this is Emily and Serena."

More and more people began getting out of their cars, greeting each other loudly. Gus made sure Serena and Emily were introduced to each of them in turn, and Emily recited their names over and over in her head, determined to remember each and every one of them.

"Please, this way," Emily said, showing the guests who had arrived into the living room for their welcome glass of wine, while Serena stayed on the porch to greet the rest.

"Oh gosh, isn't this a gorgeous room!" a woman named Sally exclaimed. "And your artwork is lovely. Is that a Turner?"

"Yes, it is," Emily replied.

"Oh, Georgia, come and look at this fireplace!" Sally exclaimed. "Real marble?"

Emily nodded as Georgia Walters joined her friend.

"I just love this lamp," Georgia added, gesturing to the Victorian brass lantern.

The two women continued to gush over the furnishings as Emily handed glasses of wine to the men, who were already sharing an apparently hilarious conversation. The house had never been so noisy. For some reason, Emily had expected her elderly guests to be timid and quiet, but they were anything but. They were downright raucous.

More and more people filed into the living room, and after fifteen minutes all twenty guests were congregated, a glass of wine in hand. All but Gus, who had a glass of port instead.

"Where's your drink, Emily?" Gus asked as he approached her, port glass in hand.

"I'm not drinking tonight," Emily replied. "I am working, after all."

"Working?" Gus exclaimed. "I'll have nothing of the sort. I want you to enjoy yourself. Relax. Join in!"

"That's very kind," Emily said, "but really, I have to stay sharp."

Gus tutted and shook his head, but he did it in a well-intended way. "Well, you've done a sterling job so far, I must say," he said, smiling. "I've never seen them so thrilled. I have a feeling this is going to be our best reunion yet."

Emily swelled with pride, though she still felt tense and apprehensive. "That's great. I'm really pleased everything is to your liking so far."

Gus was quickly distracted by another one of his friends and went off to chat.

Serena filed up to Emily. "How are you holding up?" she asked out the side of her mouth.

"So far so good," Emily said.

"They seem nice."

"They seem loud," Emily added. "We had better start checking them in. I have a feeling it's going to take quite some time to show everyone to their room."

"I think you're right," Serena said. "But there's no rush. Let's just do it one or two at a time. As soon as someone empties their glass, we'll grab them."

"That's as good a system as any," Emily said, laughing.

Emily scanned the crowd and saw that a man wearing checkered pants and a black tank top under a yellow shirt was now holding an empty glass. She went up to the ruddy-cheeked gentleman.

"Boris?" she asked, hoping she had remembered his name correctly.

"Yes, my dear," the man said.

"May I show you to your room?"

"Oh yes, yes! That would be wonderful."

Boris put his empty wine glass on the sideboard and Emily tried not to wince about the fact he hadn't used a coaster. She would have to get used to this, to people being in her home, treating it in ways she personally never would.

She leaned down and picked up Boris's heavy bag, then he followed her out of the room as she led the way. Serena had also collected a guest, a woman whom Gus had introduced as Carmel, and was struggling with what looked like an equally heavy suitcase.

Emily and Serena exchanged a smile as they headed along the corridor, muscles straining, to the staircase.

"Oh my," Boris said as Emily led him into the second room on the third floor, the one that she and Daniel had watched the storm through. "What a delightful room."

"Thank you," Emily said. She loved the room too, and couldn't quite believe that the small shell of a room had been transformed in just one day. It now had a dark wooden king-sized bed covered in the racing horse green bed set and matching throw. The furniture comprised of a wardrobe—one of Rico's antique ones made of solid walnut—bedside tables with gorgeous matching lamps on them, and a dresser with a vanity mirror on it. The rest of the smaller third-floor rooms were decorated similarly.

Boris went over to the large window and looked out at the pink clouds that spotted the streaky orange sky. "You never get tired of a Sunset Harbor sunset," he said wistfully.

He was right, and Emily couldn't help but let his words repeat over and over in her mind. She could see the love he held for Sunset Harbor in his eyes as he gazed out the window adoringly and recognized that same emotion within herself. It was something she felt strongly and often, that Sunset Harbor wasn't a place that one could grow tired of, that it had beauty and wisdom to impart on her, and lessons to teach her. More than anything in the world, Emily wanted her B&B to succeed so that she could stay here. She never wanted to become someone who wistfully longed for the Sunset Harbor sunset.

After Boris was settled in, Emily went back downstairs to continue the process of checking in the guests. Serena was right about taking their time to check them all in. No one seemed in any kind of hurry to settle down for the evening, and they wandered freely from the porch to the living room. But it ended up being for the best, and Emily and Serena grew more and more fatigued from carrying the heavy bags upstairs. It took a whole hour to get them all checked in, but finally their bags were stored away in their bedrooms and each of them had a key in their pocket.

Everyone was full of compliments, from the luxurious bedding to the beautiful antique furniture, and Emily was relieved that she'd managed to get the B&B up to standard, that no one had discovered the secret that the B&B was still in the process of being renovated that very morning, and that no one had thus far complained or demanded a refund.

The party gathered in the living room once again to go through the agenda for the weekend and enjoy an evening soiree.

Emily rejoined Serena, who was standing at the doorway looking in.

"As soon as they're in bed," Emily said, "we should get some rest too. It's going to be a really early start."

"I have a feeling they won't be sleeping for quite some time," Serena said.

She nodded her head to where Boris was settling himself down by the piano.

"Gus warned me they liked to sing," Emily said.

"Well, brace yourself," Serena replied. "Because here we go."

Boris struck some chords on the piano and within a matter of seconds the whole room erupted into song, with all the guests joining in merrily, swaying from side to side and linking arms as they sang a jaunty song about St. Matthew's.

"Maybe I should have had a port after all," Emily said to Serena.

*

The party was still in full swing at ten. By eleven, they weren't even showing signs of slowing down. At around eleven thirty, some of the group began drifting upstairs and the living room started to empty out. But it was close to midnight by the time Serena and Emily were finally able to clock off.

"Don't worry about the mess," Emily said when she saw Serena start collecting glasses. "Vanessa is coming tomorrow morning to tidy. She said she was going mad sitting at home all day with Katy and wanted to earn a few extra bucks." Emily produced the living room key from her pocket and waved it in the air. "This is a little trick that Cynthia taught me." She shepherded Serena out of the room and into the corridor and then turned and locked the door behind them. "See? Now there's no chance the guests will accidentally wander into the messy living room. All they'll see in the morning is the sparklingly clean dining room."

"Sneaky," Serena replied.

They began to climb the stairs for bed.

"Will you be okay in the office?" Emily asked Serena again. "You could always take my bed and I could go to the carriage house."

"Are you kidding me?" Serena exclaimed. "You are not leaving me here with that lot!"

Emily watched the younger woman climb the steps up to the newly renovated third floor, marveling again at how quickly it had come together. It was going to take her a while to get her head around the fact that the third floor was no longer filled with her father's dusty belongings. After so many months, the seemingly insurmountable task of sorting through his things was nearing completion.

Emily paused beside her own bedroom door. It was so strange to her now that the room had a little sign saying "Staff Only" on it, that the door was to remain locked with a key. The house felt less like a home to her now, and as much as she was enjoying the experience of hosting the B&B, she also missed the sense of belonging she had found after first restoring the house.

Emily shut and locked her bedroom door, plunging herself into darkness. She took a deep breath, letting the franticness of the day seep away from her. This morning she had woken up with one hell of a renovation job on her hands while this evening she was going to bed with a B&B filled with guests.

She dressed quietly for bed, looking out the window over the garden at the carriage house where Daniel was sleeping. She'd barely had a chance to speak to him today, other than directing him to toast more bagels and carry bits of furniture upstairs. And last night she had cut their date short because of her B&B news. Then she'd rejected him tonight, saying it felt inappropriate to have him stay over. She realized she would have to find a way to fit Daniel into her busy schedule somehow because if she didn't, the emotional distance that already sometimes existed between them could easily turn into a gulf.

Exhausted, Emily finally climbed into bed. But no sooner had she lain her head down on her pillow than she was shaken to full alertness again by a shrill sound coming from above her. It was the sound of screaming.

CHAPTER SEVENTEEN

Emily leapt out of bed and pulled her dressing gown around her as she ran out onto the landing. The lights on the third floor were already on. She rushed up the stairs to find a small group of people gathered in the hallway.

"What's happening?" Emily asked, moving toward them.

In the center of the group stood Sally, wearing nothing but a pink silky nightdress, with her hair in rollers. She looked at Emily as she nudged her way through the crowd.

"Oh, it's awful, just awful!" Sally cried.

She grabbed Emily's hand and led her into the small room. Emily immediately gagged; the room smelled disgusting.

"What is that?" she cried, covering her hand with her mouth.

"In there," Sally said, pointing toward the en suite.

Emily strode toward it and shoved the door open. The floor was soaking wet. She gasped as she realized one of the newly installed toilets had completely backed up and was flooding the room.

"OH NO!" Emily cried.

Her natural instinct was to panic, but she knew that wouldn't do anyone any good. She had to be a manager, a hostess, and that meant composing herself. She set her face and went back out into the bedroom. Sally was sitting on the bed, her hands folded in her lap.

"I'll call the plumber out right away," she said. "In the meantime, I'd like you to use my room tonight."

"Oh, I couldn't," Sally replied.

"Please," Emily said. "I insist. I can sleep in one of the spare rooms. I'll be fine."

She led Sally out into the corridor.

"It's just a problem with the plumbing," she assured the other guests. "Nothing to worry about."

They slowly went back to their own rooms.

Emily took Sally down to the second floor and whisked her into the master bedroom.

"Here, I'll get Serena to make the bed fresh for you," Emily said.

She rushed back out to find Serena. Satisfied that her guest was taken care of, Emily went downstairs and searched for the number of Barry the plumber. It was well past midnight but he answered quickly.

"I have an emergency," Emily said. "A backed up toilet. Can you help?"

"Of course," Barry replied. "I installed them in the first place. I'm so sorry. I'll fix it free of charge."

Emily hung up and took a deep breath. She couldn't believe her luck. On any other night she would have been able to put Sally up in a different bedroom, but for the toilet to back up on the one night all the guest bedrooms were occupied was just fate playing games with her!

Sitting in the dark living room, Emily shivered in her thin nightgown and tried to work out where she would sleep tonight. There always the couch, but this room had been left in complete disarray. So much for locking the door and letting Vanessa deal with the mess tomorrow. Then there was the option of calling on Daniel, but Emily didn't want to turn up at his house in the middle of the night like some damsel in distress. Plus it wouldn't be fair to Serena. What if some other disaster befell the place during the night?

Emily heard the sound of tires on gravel and rushed to the front door to see Barry parking up his van. He got out and hurried toward her.

"I'm so sorry, Emily, I don't know what could have happened," he stammered as she showed him inside.

"That doesn't matter now," Emily said. "Please just say you can get it fixed."

"Of course," Barry said. "Of course."

She showed him into the bedroom on the third floor, where Serena was desperately trying to soak up the water with old linen. In just the half hour it had taken for her to get Barry around the flood had gotten worse, and the stench was unbearable.

"Oh dear," Barry said, shaking his head. "I see what the problem is."

He pulled open his toolbox, took out a wrench, and got to work. Emily flinched at every noise he made, knowing full well it would be disturbing the guests.

Serena came over and rubbed her arm. "Are you freaking out?"

Emily nodded. "What if they all demand a refund?"

"They won't," Serena assured her. "It's just a toilet. The way that woman was screaming made it sound like she'd been visited by a ghost or something!"

Despite her tiredness and anguish, Emily couldn't help but smile. She was so glad that Serena had been around to help her out and make everything seem far less dramatic than it actually was.

Because really, if the guests did up and leave and demand a refund, well, that would be the end of everything. Emily had more or less already spent the money!

"Serena, please head back to bed," Emily said. "I'll oversee this. You've done more than enough."

Serena nodded and went back to the study to sleep.

Finally, at 1 a.m., the toilet was fixed. Emily led Barry back through the B&B silently, making sure that no one was disturbed any more than they needed to be.

Then, with no real choice, she unlocked the door to the messy living room and created a makeshift bed for herself on the couch.

*

After what felt like no more than a minute after laying her head on the cushion, her alarm was suddenly screaming at her to wake up again. Her eyes pinged open, disorientated by the fact that there was only a very dim light coming into the room, and her first thought was that her alarm had malfunctioned again. But when she grabbed it and read the time, she saw that it was indeed 5:30 and that she had to get up.

Getting up this morning was almost as difficult as it had been all those months ago when the house had been derelict and icy. She felt weary down to the very bone. Four hours of sleep was not enough for anyone to function on, let alone when it had been on a lumpy couch and after a long day of DIY and hostessing, and dressing herself was more difficult than she'd anticipated. Her hands were clumsy as she tried to button her pants. Then she put her top on the wrong way around. She stumbled about the living room, trying not to make too much noise.

Finally ready, she headed out into the hallway and went to the front door, just in time to see Vanessa's car driving up toward her. Jason's wife stepped out and waved brightly. Emily wondered how the mother of a small infant could look so much more awake than she did.

Emily kissed her friend on the cheek. "How are you so chirpy at this time of the morning?"

"Oh please, this is a lie-in for me," Vanessa said. "If you and Daniel ever have kids, I'm telling you, share feeding duties."

"I'll bear that in mind," Emily replied. She tried to smile but felt a tug in her chest at the possibility of never being able to have kids with Daniel because they were constantly going from one disaster with the B&B to the next, either just scraping by financially or finally tanking and having to give everything up. She couldn't help but wonder whether they'd ever have the sort of stability needed to bring a child into the world.

Emily showed Vanessa into the living room.

"Oh my," Vanessa said. "It looks like a bomb went off in here. I thought you said on the phone that it was just twenty elderly folk coming."

"They turned out to be rowdier than I was expecting," Emily said, glancing around at the empty wine glasses strewn all over the place.

"Lucky I'm here!" Vanessa said.

Emily thanked her, then left her to get to work tidying up the room. As she stepped into the corridor, she noticed Daniel just coming in through the main door with two eggs in his hands.

"Gifts from Lola and Lolly," he said, holding them up. Then he planted a kiss on Emily's cheek. "And that's a gift from me."

She smiled at him. "Good morning," she said as they walked together to the kitchen. "Did you sleep well last night?"

"Better than you by the looks of things," he replied.

"Hey," Emily said. "You're supposed to tell me I look delightful."

Daniel rolled his eyes. "You know I think you look delightful. I mean that you look tired *as well as* delightful. Did they keep you up late? The lights were all still on when I got home."

They reached the kitchen and, as Emily went over to the coffee machine to brew a fresh batch, she couldn't help but feel suspicious about what Daniel had said.

"Yes, they were up until after midnight. How come you were out late?" She tried to make the question sound innocent enough but could hear the edge of worry in her own tone.

"I went for a bike ride on the cliffs," Daniel said.

"Until after midnight?"

"Yup."

Emily kept her focus on preparing the coffee machine, but her mind was ticking overtime at the thought of Daniel needing to be on the move, always on the move, never settled. If she'd had an evening to herself, she would have relaxed at home and enjoyed the splendor of the home she'd created. But Daniel had used it as an opportunity to get out and about, to explore. Nothing exhilarated him more than being on the move. For not the first time, Emily worried about whether their relationship would ever take root.

Emily finished putting on the coffee. "I'd better get the curtains open," she said, immediately leaving the room to get a bit of space.

"I'll help," Daniel said brightly.

She didn't say a word as he followed her around, opening up the curtains in the downstairs rooms so the place would be bright and inviting when the guests awoke for breakfast.

"So how did it go last night, then?" Daniel asked as they went back into the kitchen for coffee. "You never told me."

"It was good," she said, sounding a tad irritable. "They all seemed happy enough. They drank wine, they sang songs. That's the long and short of it."

"Oh," Daniel said as he handed her a mug of coffee. "Okay."

"Sorry, I've barely slept," Emily said, trying to shrug off her mood. "One of the toilets broke so I had Barry out doing emergency repairs and then I had to put one of the guests in my room so I slept on the couch."

It was true that she was too tired for conversation, but she was also getting caught up in her anxiety about her relationship with Daniel. She reasoned it was the stress of the last few days making her grumpy and exacerbating her anxiety. She practically fell into a chair and huddled over her coffee.

Just then, Serena bounded into the room looking as fresh faced as ever. She beamed as she helped herself to a cup of coffee.

"So, I stayed up late looking at all the artwork you have stored in the office," she said. "You should really think about displaying some of it. There's one of a lighthouse at night. It's very atmospheric."

Those damn lighthouse portraits, Emily thought to herself. She hadn't wanted to throw any of them out since they clearly held some kind of significance to her father and might possibly hold some clues into his disappearance, so she'd stored them all in his office. But the last thing she wanted to think about now was her father eloping with the artist.

"Maybe," she said with a shrug. "I mean, you're an artist. If you think it would look better in here with some art, by all means go ahead."

"Cool," Serena said, beaming, clearly not picking up on the sharpness in Emily's tone. "I'll hang it in the dining room."

Just then, Emily heard the sound of the back door opening and in strolled Parker Black. She glanced over at the clock, her eyes still bleary with sleep, and saw that it was six o'clock on the dot. Emily couldn't help her surprise; she'd been certain he would turn up at least five minutes late.

"Parker?" Emily said, failing to keep the sound of surprise from her voice.

"That's me," he said in the confident manner she expected of him. "And you don't need to look so shocked. Have I ever given you a reason to have such little faith in me?"

Before Emily had a chance to answer, Parker strolled into the kitchen and helped himself to coffee. Then he hopped up onto the counter, looking very much at home, like he was part of the team. Emily looked from Serena to Daniel to Parker, wondering how she had assembled such a motley crew.

Just then, somewhere through the sound of Vanessa's vacuum cleaner in the living room, Emily heard something coming from high above her that sounded like a bedroom door being unlocked.

"Someone's coming down for breakfast," she said.

Everyone looked at her, frowning.

"How do you know that?" Daniel asked.

"I can hear someone moving around," Emily replied, straining to hear better.

"I can't hear a thing," Parker said.

"Maybe she's developed that thing that new moms get," Serena said, grinning widely, "where they wake up if their baby so much as coughs at night, but will sleep through the fire alarm."

Parker laughed.

"You should ask Vanessa," Daniel said.

"Shh!" Emily exclaimed. "Listen, will you?" Just then, she heard the creaking of floorboards coming from the second floor. "It's one of the second floor guests. It could be Gus." She'd put Gus in the main bedroom, Mr. Kapowski's room, since if it hadn't been for him she'd never have gotten any guests at all. "We'd better get ready," Emily added.

"Get ready how?" Daniel said, raising an eyebrow.

"I don't know. Smooth down our clothes. Stand up straight." She waved at Parker, who was still sitting languorously on the worktop.

He leapt down with a shrug. Serena stifled a giggle.

Despite the success of the evening, Emily felt the same fluttering butterflies in her stomach. This was a whole new thing for her, making breakfast for so many people, and she'd managed to make a mess of serving just the one for Mr. Kapowski. Once again she felt that sensation of complete inadequacy, like she was woefully underprepared.

Daniel must have sensed her panic. He came over and rested his hands on her shoulders.

"Are you okay, Emily?" he asked gently. "You seem a bit off this morning."

She nodded and tried to let go of some of the niggling worry she was carrying around with her. She took some deep breaths. "I just want it to be perfect for them."

Daniel kissed her forehead. "It is. You're doing a great job."

She felt relieved to get some physical affection from Daniel. She knew she shouldn't doubt him so much, but her parents' divorce and dad's disappearance, not to mention all her previous failed relationships, sometimes made her expect the worst from people. Just because Daniel wanted to ride his motorcycle up on the cliffs all night didn't mean he was about to run off and leave her unannounced.

Emily heard the creaking of floorboards underfoot and could tell that her guest was now on the bottom staircase, heading downstairs. She put on her game face and went out into the corridor to greet them.

It was Sally, the woman who had been woken by the leaking toilet.

"Oh," Emily said. "You're up early. Did you sleep okay after I changed your room?"

"Oh yes," Sally said. "My bed was gloriously comfortable. I don't think I've slept as well in years."

"That's what I like to hear," Emily replied, relieved that the old woman appeared to be in no way disgruntled by the whole debacle. "Your toilet has been fixed now so you'll be able to return to your room tonight."

"That sounds most delightful, my dear," Sally said.

Emily led her into the dining room to make her a coffee while she waited for the others. Despite Cynthia's advice to remove the table and fill the space with smaller café-style tables so the guests could dine separately, Emily had kept the original layout. Her hope was to one day convert one of the outer buildings into a conservatory, knock through a wall, and expand the dining room outward that way. But for now, she had left everything the way it was, with one large table like the type you'd see in a stately home.

"Gosh, what a wonderful room!" Sally exclaimed. "And all that light," she added, turning to look at the large open windows that no longer had a view straight onto the chicken coop, but all the gorgeous flower beds that Daniel had created instead.

"Thank you," Emily said. "This is one of my favorite rooms. Actually," she added, thoughtfully, "I can't pick a favorite. They all are."

Sally laughed as she took her seat at the dining table. Emily left the room to fetch her coffee but bumped into Gus in the hallway.

"Gus," she said, her voice sounding worried, "I am so sorry about what happened last night."

"Nonsense," Gus replied, jovially. "A minor problem which you resolved very quickly indeed. Nothing to worry about at all."

Emily was beyond grateful for how relaxed he was being about the whole thing.

For some reason, Gus never failed to put a smile on Emily's face. Perhaps it was his upbeat attitude and the fact that he smiled easily and laughed readily. Emily often found herself drawn to such people, the ones who joked and laughed, who were able to hold a room with their tales. Emily herself tended to stick to the background, to be the observer of situations rather than the leader within them. It wasn't a trait she particularly liked about herself, especially since it was part of the reason why she ended up in such terrible relationships, letting herself be dragged around by someone else's whims.

Gus settled in beside Sally, and Emily left to fetch them both a mug of coffee. When she entered the kitchen she found Serena and Parker goofing around.

"Hey," she said. "Serena, can you go out into the corridor, please? Direct the guests to the dining room. Parker, you should be scrubbed up already and in your apron."

The two youngsters exchanged a glance before leaping to attention. That was the first time Emily had really had to *manage* anyone before. It felt very strange to her but at the same time not altogether unpleasant. She wondered whether she really could get used to running a B&B.

Once the rest of the guests had woken up and filed downstairs into the dining room, Serena and Emily took all their breakfast orders. The guests were just as rowdy at seven in the morning as they were at eleven at night and it took quite a while to get everything down. Finally, the two women went into the kitchen.

"Okay," Emily said, reading off the pad. "We need ten portions of poached eggs with baked salmon and toast, five smoked salmons with scrambled eggs and toast, two eggs benedicts—one with spinach, one with bacon—and three fried eggs with bacon and toast." She took a deep breath. "Then for drinks we need ten coffees, five orange juices, four iced teas, and one glass of milk for Gus. Let's go."

They got straight to work, boiling water for the eggs, toasting and buttering the bread, baking the salmon.

"Why don't you let us handle this?" Daniel said to Emily when they were well underway. "You should be out there with the guests doing the hostess thing."

"Good idea," Emily said. She picked up the coffee pot. "I'll fill them up while I'm at it. Not that they need any more stimulation, to be honest with you. I've never seen such an energetic bunch in my life!"

Daniel laughed, and Emily backed out of the kitchen into the corridor. Vanessa was just coming out of the living room.

"All done?" Emily asked.

"Not quite, I just wanted to grab you to ask whether you'd like me to also help clean the kitchen after breakfast and the bedrooms once the guests have left for the day? I don't mind sticking around until eleven or so."

"Wow, it really must be tough being a mom if you'd prefer to be here cleaning than at home!" Emily joked.

"You have no idea," Vanessa said. "But you'll get it once you have little ones yourself."

Emily tried to smile through the anguish that rippled in her whenever Vanessa made suggestions about motherhood.

"Well, if you really don't have to rush back," Emily said. "I could definitely do with the extra hands."

Vanessa shook her head. "Jason has taken Katy and the dogs for a long walk up in Acadia Park anyway. I would just be going home to an empty house."

"Okay," Emily agreed. "It would be great if you stayed. Feel free to help yourself to coffee and breakfast if you get hungry."

Vanessa went back into the living room to finish vacuuming and Emily entered the dining room, coffee pot in hand.

"And here's the liquid black energy!" Gus cried. He pumped his fist against the tabletop. "Fill me up please, Emily!"

Emily still didn't understand how the old man had such exuberance at this time of the morning, let alone at his age, but she topped up his mug nonetheless.

"Excuse me, young lady," one of the guests said to Emily as she topped up her coffee.

"Yes, it's Georgia, isn't it?" Emily said.

"Yes, what a splendid memory you have," Georgia replied, the steam from her mug coiling around her. "Now, this may seem like a strange question, but I couldn't help wondering whether you might be related to Roy Mitchell?"

"Yes," Emily gasped, surprised to hear her father's name. "I'm his daughter. Did you know him?"

The woman seemed delighted to have made the connection. "Oh yes! Well, I lived in Sunset Harbor for many years before moving out of Maine about, well, it must have been thirty years ago now. We were in the same hiking group, you see. I was much more of an avid enthusiast. Your father was more of the occasional ambler." She laughed.

Emily took the new slice of information about her father's life and tried to slot it in next to all the other things she was discovering about him.

"Your father just loved it here," Georgia continued. "Well, here and Barcelona, of course."

She chuckled, but Emily felt a sensation like ice sweep through her. This was the second person who had mentioned that her father had a love of Barcelona. Just a few weeks ago she hadn't even been aware of this particular interest of his at all. Even after having looked through so much of his paperwork she hadn't found any evidence of it!

Emily didn't want to get lost in her speculative thoughts but she couldn't help it. She'd found so much stuff belonging to her dad—from bank statements to credit card bills to old address books to receipts for lawn seed—how could she have missed something as significant as his love of Barcelona? It must have been an important enough part of his life for an acquaintance from his hiking group to know about it, so how could it not have been evident, somewhere, amongst his things? There was nothing, not a boarding pass for an airplane, not a booking reservation for a hotel, not even a fridge magnet. Could it be there was no evidence because her dad had specifically disposed of it? Because he was planning on running away to Barcelona twenty years ago and hadn't wanted anyone, not even her, to ever find a trace of him?

Emily became suddenly aware that Georgia was still speaking.

"You will tell him hello from Georgia Walters next time you see him, won't you?" she was saying. "Say, where did he move to in the end? I assume he moved house because he suddenly stopped coming on our walks."

Emily shook her head. "I… um—"

"Oh," Georgia said, looking at Emily's pale face. "Have I said something out of line?" She touched Emily's hand lightly with her cool, soft hands.

Emily tried to get a grip on herself, but the thoughts were swirling. She felt as though the mystery of her father's disappearance had acquired a whole new facet in the last few weeks and she was trying to wrap her head around the fact that there was another place her father used to disappear to that wasn't Sunset Harbor. Could it really be that one day he'd just decided that he wanted to live out his life on the beach in the sunshine and leave his daughter behind?

"Excuse me, please," Emily said breathlessly, drawing her hand out from under the woman's and rushing away.

She went into the kitchen, shoving the door hard. The room was a flurry of noise and activity. Steam permeated the air and the smell of cooked salmon wafted up her nostrils. The heat was almost suffocating.

"Hey," Daniel said, turning as she entered. "I thought you were out there hostessing."

"Serena," Emily said, ignoring him, "can you take over, please?"

Serena looked concerned. "Sure," she said, wiping her hands on her apron before pulling it over her head and handing it to Emily.

Daniel came over to her, spatula in hand, dripping oil onto the tiles. "What's wrong?"

Emily shook her head and took the spatula out of his grasp. "Nothing. I'm just… I'm freaking out a bit."

"You're doing fine," Daniel reassured her.

Emily grabbed some paper towels from the counter and began mopping up the oil spills. "It's not that," she said as she worked.

"It looks like that to me," Daniel replied, bending down and taking the paper towels from her hands before taking over wiping up the oil. "Looks like you might be overworking yourself."

"One of the guests knew my dad, okay?" Emily snapped. "She just said something that's messed with my head a bit. I'll be fine. I just need some air."

She stood hurriedly, leaving Daniel crouched on the floor looking bemused. She could feel his concerned eyes on her as she walked out of the uncomfortably hot kitchen. She knew he was worried that she was either going to hyperventilate again like she had when her mom had visited or black out into one of her weird memory flashbacks, and she hated feeling so fragile, hated knowing that her past experiences could affect the present moment so profoundly.

Once outside, Emily rested her back against the wall and breathed in the ocean air.

"Did you want a smoke?" someone said, and Emily leapt a mile. She glanced over and saw Boris. He was offering a cigarette to her.

"No, thanks," Emily said. Then she added in a mocking tone, "I came out for *fresh* air."

Boris smirked. "Have we already given you a headache?"

Emily smiled and shook her head. "Not at all. You're a delight to have around."

Boris took a final puff of his cigarette before dropping it to the ground and smooshing it under his foot. "Well, I must say, of all the hotels and B&Bs we've stayed in over the years, this has got to be one of the best. I can feel the love and attention that's gone into it. It feels more like a family home than a B&B in a way."

"It was a family home," Emily told him. "My father's, in fact. I would spend my summers here."

"Lucky you," Boris said. He smiled and went back inside.

Emily quickly picked up his cigarette butt and reminded herself she would have to get ashtrays. She threw the butt away in the trash and went back inside to help serve breakfast.

"You okay?" Daniel asked when she returned.

"I'll be fine. Stop worrying about me." Emily picked up the first two plates of food. "These look really great. Much better than the breakfast I served Mr. Kapowski. Good job."

She went back into the dining room, where she found Serena taking photographs of the guests as they shouted directions at her. "And now one with Carmel! And this time with the garden in the background!"

"Your breakfasts are ready," she announced.

Everyone cheered and took their seats again. Emily served the first two plates to Georgia and Gus.

"I'm very sorry if I said anything to upset you," Georgia said as she took the breakfast plate from Emily.

Emily shook her head. "I was just a little shocked that you knew my father. He's not with us anymore, sadly. But I'd love to hear any stories you have of him at some point."

Georgia nodded and Emily left to collect the next set of plates.

Once everyone had some food, Vanessa joined the others in the kitchen so they could quickly fuel up on coffee and toast. Emily could hardly comprehend the level of mess that had been created. She hadn't really thought she'd need an extra cleaner with the four of them already on board but now she could see she had underestimated the amount of mess that a full B&B could really generate.

Emily checked her watch to discover that 9 a.m. had already arrived and the breakfast shift was over.

"Let's tidy up their plates," she said to Serena. "See if that prompts them to get a move on."

They returned to the dining room and began collecting plates. As they did so, Gus spoke loudly to the group about their agenda for the day.

"A hike in the park and a picnic lunch. Then back here so those of us who need them can have an afternoon nap—I'm looking at you, Boris—before dinner at the yacht club. Then it's down to the beach for a bonfire and Fourth of July fireworks."

Everyone let out a cheer of excitement and Emily suddenly realized what date it was. She'd been so wrapped up in her work that she'd forgotten about how she'd needed to fill the B&B by the Fourth of July. Yet here she was having accomplished just that!

Her own excitement bubbled through her as she realized just how close she was to reaching her goal of a maxed out B&B on the Fourth July.

She and Serena finished carrying the plates back into the kitchen as Gus and his group donned their walking boots in their typically noisy fashion. Emily started to feel a bit like she was herding sheep as she watched them chaotically try to get themselves organized for the day trip.

Soon she was waving them off from the front porch, listening to their merry chatter fade away to silence. She walked back into the B&B, struck immediately by the hush that had fallen over it like a blanket of snow. Now that it was quiet, Emily could tell that her ears were ringing.

She went into the kitchen to find everyone slumped at the kitchen table. She clapped her hands and they all flinched up.

"Right, we have twenty bedrooms to clean. Twenty sets of beds to make. Twenty lots of bathroom supplies, toilet rolls, and towels to replenish. We need to vacuum and dust twenty bedrooms, mop twenty en suites, and scrub twenty toilets. And we've only got until after lunch to do it."

"When they'll be back to mess it all up again," Serena added wryly.

"Well, at least they only get room service once a day," Emily added. "Come on. Let's go. We can rest once everything's done. Except you, Vanessa," she said. "You just go whenever you need to."

"That's not fair," Parker said. "How come I can't go whenever I want?"

"You can," Emily said. "Work for as long as you want to earn for. That's the deal."

Parker shut his mouth and everyone went off to complete their assigned tasks. All, that is, except for Daniel.

"Emily," Daniel said the second they were alone. She could hear the warning in his voice.

"Yes?"

"Do you need to slow down a bit? Maybe take some time to rest?"

Emily shook her head. "Nope. I think I need to do the opposite. Work hard, party hard."

Daniel gave her a worried look, but Emily was having none of it. Not this weekend. She strolled out of the kitchen, leaving Daniel behind.

CHAPTER EIGHTEEN

Emily watched the second hand of her clock as it ticked closer and closer to midnight. "Three... two... one... Happy Fourth of July!"

Daniel swept her up in his arms and planted a kiss on her lips. "You did it." He beamed. "The Inn at Sunset Harbor is still open for business." He set Emily down on her feet. "Now, can I *please* have you to myself for a little while?"

"I'm sorry I've been so busy," Emily replied. "But I promise I am all yours. Until six a.m., that is."

"Good," Daniel said, grabbing her hand. "Then you'd better come with me."

Emily flashed him a curious smile as he led her out to the porch. It was a balmy evening, and the sky was bright with color from the fireworks being set off around town. As she stood there gazing up at the sky, Emily felt herself being transported back to another time.

"Happy Fourth of July, Emily Jane," her father said. He swept her up in his arms and placed her on his hip. "Let's go upstairs. There's something amazing I want you to see."

He carried her up the long staircase to the second floor then up again, all the way to the third floor. They never came up here, and it felt unfamiliar to her with its cobwebs and old furniture. Then her dad carried her all the way along the corridor to a small door at the end. He pulled the door and it opened with a creak. Behind it was a small spiral staircase. Emily held on tightly as he began to ascend the dark staircase. Then suddenly a blast of air hit Emily's face and she gasped.

"This is the best view you're going to get in the whole of Sunset Harbor," her dad said.

They were standing on the rooftops, on a platform with a metal railing. Emily clung even more tightly around her father's neck as she looked down at the wide ocean. Emily could also see all the people on the beach and little glowing bonfires burning on the sand. Just then there was a loud squealing sound. Emily screamed as the squeal turned into an enormous bang, and she buried her face against her father.

"Hush," he said in her ear, rocking her gently. "There's nothing to be afraid of Emily Jane." He tried to remove her hands from her eyes but Emily stubbornly refused. "Come on, sweetheart. Look. It's noisy but it's very pretty."

116

He finally managed to coax her out of her fear. The next boom made her flinch but she didn't cover her eyes this time. She gasped as colors exploded across the sky.

"Fireworks," her dad said as he bounced her on his hip. "They're pretty, aren't they?"

All Emily could do was gasp in wonder as the beautiful colored lights cracked and fizzed against the black sky, their beauty reflected in the dark ocean water. She snuggled against her dad, laughing merrily and clapping at every burst of color.

"They're beautiful, aren't they?" a voice said in her ear.

Not her father's anymore, but Daniel's. She was back in the present time, her childhood memory fading away.

Daniel wrapped his arms around her from behind. "You just had another blackout," he told her. There was a tone to his voice that almost seemed to say *I told you so.*

But Emily didn't mind. That was the first happy flashback she'd ever had, the first one that had made her feel warm and loved. It wasn't an awful one brought on by extreme anguish or stress. It was the sort of memory she welcomed; one that reminded her of the wonderful man her father had been. It was like an antidote to all the troubling thoughts she'd been having about him.

"I flashed back to the first time I ever saw fireworks," Emily said, holding the memory in her mind as gently as a fragile gift. She made a mental note to check to see whether there was a concealed door in the attic leading out to a widow's walk.

"You don't seem as upset as usual," Daniel noted.

"I'm not," she said in agreement. "It was a good one. A happy one."

She felt Daniel tighten his arms around her and realized how much she'd missed his touch. Over the last few months they'd gotten used to being with each other all the time, following their own routines. Not once since their relationship began had there been such a huge barrier between them. Even if it had only been two days, it had felt so long since they'd touched one another.

"Come with me," Daniel said suddenly, grabbing her hand.

"Where are we going?" Emily laughed.

But Daniel didn't say a word as he pulled her along the garden path. Purples and blues exploded in the sky, illuminating the garden, turning the flowers strange colors.

"Now, wait here just one second," Daniel said when they reached the end of the driveway.

He disappeared toward his carriage house and returned moments later carrying a bag.

"And what is that?" Emily asked, her curiosity mounting.

"You'll find out soon enough." Daniel grinned.

Then he steered Emily out of the driveway, across the street, and onto the path that led to the beach.

When they reached the sand, Daniel laced his fingers through Emily's. They strolled together, hand in hand, as fireworks exploded in the sky above them. Emily took in a deep, satisfied breath, feeling content despite her fatigue.

"I think this is as good a spot as any," Daniel said, gesturing to a small circle of rocks.

He slung the bag off his back and set it down in the sand. For the first time, Emily got a glimpse of what was inside. Chocolate. Marshmallows. Kindling to make a fire.

"Oh, Daniel," she gasped, touched by the romantic gesture.

Daniel cobbled together a small fire and they both settled down beside it on the rocks.

"So what does it feel like having the house full of guests?" Daniel asked Emily a moment later as he handed her a crisp, toasted marshmallow.

"Strange," she admitted. "But I like it. Not the sleeping on the couch part so much," she added with a smile.

"Maybe you should stay with me in the carriage house next time," Daniel replied.

Emily took a bite of marshmallow. "I wouldn't want to get in the way of your midnight cliff rides," she said, struggling to hide her suspicions.

Daniel gave her a look. "You wouldn't be in the way. I just need a bit of space sometimes. Space to ride my bike or go for a sail. I need a lot of time to clear my head, that's all."

Emily nodded. She understood that Daniel had such needs but she had needs too—to know where he was, for starters.

"Do you think you could maybe keep me up to speed?" she said. "Like drop me a text?"

Daniel laughed. "With what cell phone?"

"Oh yeah," Emily replied, remembering Daniel's hatred of all things electronic. "Well, just leave me a note or something. I can't cope when you disappear on me. What with my past, with my dad. And especially after last time."

Daniel grew quiet. "I'm sorry," he said earnestly. "Truly. I won't disappear on you like that again. But I need you to trust me." He reached out and took her hand. "Because what we're doing here feels really good to me."

"Me too," Emily replied, her voice small and timid. "Which is what makes it so hard when you disappear like that."

Daniel nodded, seeming to understand. "So," he said, getting the conversation back on track, "next time you have a full B&B, will you stay at mine instead of on the couch?" He nudged her playfully with his shoulder. "Because when the B&B picks up you can't be expected to sleep there every single night. You're still allowed a personal life."

Emily smiled to herself. It always warmed her when Daniel spoke of the future because it meant he could envision himself in her life for at least the foreseeable future. With Daniel, that was about as much as she could hope for in the way of commitment.

"I'll try and balance my work and personal life a little better next time."

"Next time or this time?" Daniel teased.

"Okay, okay!" Emily laughed, relenting. "You can stay over."

"Good," Daniel said, satisfied. He reached over and kissed her deeply on the lips. "Because I don't want to have to fight Gus for you."

At that, they both dissolved into laughter.

CHAPTER NINETEEN

The next day, everyone was weary, staff and guests alike. Everyone seemed to have been up partying and seeing in the Fourth of July. But despite that, breakfast was another resounding success. In fact, everything seemed to delight Gus and his reunion party, from Parker's eggs benedict to the Denby coffee mugs. Emily was glad to see her guests so happy and took each of their compliments readily.

Then Emily waved them off for their next day of planned festivities, feeling a bit like a parent trying to get their children out of the house for the day.

As soon as they were gone, Emily climbed the stairs quickly, more than ready to slip back beneath the covers and snuggle up next to Daniel. Only, as she checked her phone by the door, she saw she had a notification. She picked it up, scrolling past the numerous missed calls from Ben that had flared up again recently, and saw that there was an eBay alert on her phone. She read it quickly then squealed with excitement before rushing back upstairs.

"Daniel, I got an eBay alert for the roofing tiles we need," she said all in a rush. "There's a place in Portland that's selling them for a fraction of the price the roofer quoted. If we get them, we could pay him just to replace the beams and do the labor! I'd be able to get the whole roof replaced using the money from the diamond and the guests." She leaped back into bed next to him, as excited as a kid on Christmas. "I know it's not very romantic," she added giving him an apologetic look. "But we can still make a date of it."

Emily could sense Daniel's reluctance. But at the same time, getting the roof repaired for a fifth of the price she was expecting wasn't exactly something she could turn her nose up at.

"Let me guess," he said, finally, yawning. "I'm driving."

"Well," Emily said, "we'll need to use your pickup truck and I can't drive a stick shift, so…"

"Of course," Daniel replied. "I'll be driving and you'll be snoozing."

"How dare you!" Emily laughed.

They both dressed and then headed out of the house and down the driveway to where Daniel's pickup truck was parked outside his carriage house. Emily could feel tiredness clinging to her like a lead weight as she leaped into the passenger side of the truck. Daniel turned the ignition and the truck rumbled to life.

Daniel took the coastal route to Portland. Despite her tiredness, Emily couldn't resist watching the glittering water, and cooing admiringly at the pretty towns that neighbored Portland.

"It's really beautiful around here," Emily said.

"It is," Daniel agreed. "But it's about to get decidedly less beautiful while we detour to this parking lot."

He pulled off the pretty coastal road and onto the busy interstate. A few minutes later they were in the heart of the city, with noisy traffic racing past them, making Emily cringe as she remembered her hectic New York lifestyle. Daniel parked, and they both got out of the truck and went up to the door of an apartment building. Emily shivered in the shadow it cast across the asphalt.

Daniel pressed the buzzer and told the voice over the intercom that they were there to pick up the slate tiles. A moment later the front door of the apartment opened and a guy wearing a white tank top stretched over a portly belly walked out.

"I picked these up at a flea market," he said, leading them around to a garage at the back of the block where a black tarpaulin covered the heap of slate tiles. "Figured they'd be worth something to someone. That's you guys, right?" He grinned.

Emily couldn't help but find the whole encounter a little uncomfortable and wanted it over with as soon as possible. The man had clearly gotten lucky with the find, and they in turn had gotten lucky that he didn't appreciate their full worth.

There were enough slate tiles for the entire roof replacement. Daniel began lugging them into the back of the truck while Emily exchanged money with the man.

"You guys can handle the loading?" he asked as he thumbed the dollar bills in his hands, clearly not about to offer any help.

"Yeah," Daniel said, grimacing with the strain of lifting yet more heavy tiles into the truck.

"We'll be fine," Emily replied as she picked up a stack with a groan.

The man disappeared back into his apartment building, leaving Emily and Daniel with the arduous, heavy-lifting work.

"So when does the date part start?" Emily grimaced as she wiped the sweat from her brow.

Daniel heaped the last of the tiles into the truck and let out a long exhalation. "How about now?"

Emily smiled, glad that there was no more heavy lifting to do.

"Great," she said.

They got back into the truck and Daniel turned the engine on. "Where do you want to go?" he asked.

"Why don't you show me where you grew up?" Emily said.

"Really?" Daniel asked in a tone that suggested he couldn't work out whether she was being serious or not. "I mean you just saw that apartment complex. It's not much better than that."

Emily frowned. "I want to see where you grew up. Please!"

Daniel seemed more than a little hesitant.

"Please please please," Emily said. "I want to know more about your childhood. You've met my friends and my mom and seen my emotional breakdowns, but I know next to nothing about you."

Daniel raised an eyebrow. "You wanna see where I grew up? Fine. Let's go."

He revved the engine and drove them out of the parking lot, back along the busy city roads. After a while he turned onto a small street with some sad-looking houses. It was completely dilapidated, the sort of place where children played barefoot in the street and Rottweilers chained to fences barked angrily.

"It's actually looking better than it did when I grew up here," Daniel said when he saw Emily's expression.

"I had no idea," she gasped, looking around at the signs of deprivation: a trash can on its side, litter blowing in the breeze. "How long did you live here for?" She spoke gently, sensing Daniel's somber mood and feeling guilty for having been the one to cause it.

"Not long. My parents divorced when I was pretty young. Five, I think. So yeah, only until then. We lived in a bunch of different places in Maine after that. Dad moved to Sunset Harbor so I started to see that as some kind of refuge, even though he was drunk all the time. But he didn't seem to care too much what I got up to, and when you're a teenager that seems pretty great. My poor mom, though, when I think back to what I put her through."

Emily listened patiently. She knew very little about Daniel's past; he was usually so stoic and secretive. That he was opening up to her now seemed like a small miracle.

Daniel pointed through the windshield toward a solitary tree growing out of the sidewalk. It was a birch tree, with a bare, silver trunk pocked with dark whorls.

"That's where I was standing when my dad left," Daniel said, his voice quiet, a wounded tone vibrating in his throat. "For the last time. The final time. He'd gone before, threatened to almost every day." A sad smile flicked across his lips. "But that time felt different. I was just a kid but I knew that it was the end. I watched him get in his car and drive up the road and out of sight. Then I just stayed there, watching, like I thought maybe if I stood there long enough he'd turn around and come back. Mom couldn't get me to come inside. I stood there hugging that damn tree all night."

Emily watched as he tipped his gaze down to his lap, his shoulders hunched over. She'd never seen him look so resigned, so filled with pain.

"I'm sorry for making you come here," Emily said. "I shouldn't have been so insistent."

Daniel reached out and patted her arm. "Actually, I think it was good to come here. Cathartic." He looked at her earnestly. "I've never told anyone that before."

Emily could tell that Daniel was telling the truth. Seeing his home and sharing that part of himself with her had actually been good for him. Therapeutic. But that didn't stop him from clamming up all over again. She could almost see the moment his eyes clouded over again, as though shying away from the pain of his past, blocking it out so as not to get too close to it. Emily understood; she herself had spent years running from the trauma of her own childhood.

"Why don't we head back home?" Emily suggested. "Go on a proper date. We could head out in your boat again. We haven't had a chance to go out in it together since Memorial Day."

Daniel smiled at her. "Okay," he said, sounding touched that she was making such an effort at reparation. "That sounds great."

"It's a date," Emily replied.

This time, she really hoped it would be.

*

As soon as they returned home, Emily went upstairs to prepare herself for her date with Daniel. She felt bad about how the morning had gone, not to mention the last few days, and wanted to make up for it.

She dolled herself up, putting on one of her nicest dresses and doing her hair.

As soon as she was ready, she raced down the stairs and opened the door. She slammed straight into a woman standing on the porch. The woman was young, with dry, dyed platinum-blond hair that hung well past her shoulders. She had a tight black leather jacket on and pale blue jeans that accentuated her long, slim legs.

"I'm so sorry," Emily said, apologizing for having bumped into the woman. "Can I help you?"

"Uh, yeah," the woman said, slightly hesitantly. She seemed on edge, Emily noted. "I was wondering if Daniel was here."

At the sound of his name Emily paused. Her brain seemed to take a while to connect the dots. There'd been rumors in town of Daniel having a past with women, something he'd assured her was well and truly in the past.

"Daniel?" Emily said, warily, noting the tremble of fear vibrating in her stomach.

The woman scratched her neck and shifted her weight from one foot to the other. "Did I get the right address?" the woman said, worrying a piece of paper with the address of the carriage house scrawled on it in her hands.

This time when she spoke, Emily noticed her sweet, summery, southern accent. She knew Daniel had spent time in Tennessee in his youth. It was where he'd gotten into trouble with the law after defending a girlfriend from her abusive partner.

"Yes, that's the right address," Emily said.

All at once, she felt herself turn very cold. The sun was shining brightly but she might as well have been standing on a snowy mountain side. It began to dawn on her that this woman standing on her porch was someone from Daniel's past.

"I'm sorry," Emily said, her voice beginning to waver. "But who are you?"

"My name's Sheila," she young woman said finally. "I'm his girlfriend."

CHAPTER TWENTY

Emily felt like a chasm had opened up inside of her. She stood on the porch, stunned, feeling suddenly ridiculous for being all dolled up for a date night.

"Girlfriend?" she repeated, her voice barely more than a whisper.

Just then, she noticed Daniel striding up the garden path. He'd gone to some effort with his outfit too, something that he never usually did, and was looking more handsome than ever, with the warm yellow light spilling out from the B&B dancing across his features. Seeing him sent a jolt of pain lancing through Emily.

Their eyes met for a moment and he smiled. Then Emily watched as the smile began to fade from his eyes before disappearing entirely as it dawned on him who it was standing on the porch with her. Daniel strode toward them, his face transforming into one of fury. By the time he reached them he was completely pale.

"Hi, sugar," Sheila said in her sickly sweet southern accent.

Emily felt herself boiling inside.

"What are you doing here?" Daniel demanded, his tone frosty.

"I came to see you, silly," Sheila said.

Emily finally found her tongue. "I'll leave you two to catch up," she said with terse derision, then turned to head for the door.

"Emily, wait," Daniel barked, his voice sounding more desperate than she'd ever heard it before. "I can explain."

She paused and glanced over her shoulder. Daniel was looking at her appealingly, an emotion somewhere between anguish and grief on his face. Usually his face could melt her heart—she was never able to stay mad at him—but this time was different. This time he'd taken her trust and trampled it to pieces.

"Oh, I bet you can," she shot back, her voice acidic. "I bet you think you can smooth talk your way out of this like you smooth talked your way out of all my other fears and concerns. But now I find out I had a legitimate reason to be worried! Is this who you were seeing when you were off 'riding your bike' until midnight? I'm such an idiot for falling for that! All that quietness and clamming up, I just thought I had to be patient."

She could feel the heat in her cheeks, the anger rising through her. Anger at herself for falling for Daniel, for forcing herself to trust him and go against her instincts. She'd been vulnerable after breaking up with Ben and had let another man into her life to walk all over her.

She turned on her heel, again, heading back into the house. But this time Daniel grabbed her arm, stopping her in her tracks.

"Emily! Please!"

"Get off!" she cried, livid.

She wrenched herself free and, as she did, caught sight of Sheila standing there with a hint of smugness on her lips. It was almost as though she was enjoying herself, was getting a kick out of Emily's distress.

"Why don't you go off with your tart, Daniel!" she shouted.

Sheila made a mock-insulted expression. "Excuse me! Daniel, are you going to let her talk like that to the mother of your child?"

In that moment, the world seemed to stop. Silence descended, so thick Emily could almost touch it. It felt like someone had punched her in the gut.

"You have a kid?" she stammered.

"No," Daniel protested. "That's not true!"

"Yes, it is!" Sheila exclaimed. "We have a kid, Daniel." Then her voice softened. "You're a daddy. Surprise." She smiled weakly.

Emily watched as Daniel stood there dumbfounded. Her mind was swirling with confusion. She couldn't make sense of what she was hearing. All she knew was that she didn't want to be there anymore. She had heard quite enough.

"Sounds like you two have some catching up to do," she said in a somber whisper.

Then she opened the door and walked inside, leaving Daniel floundering on the porch. The second she was inside and concealed from view, she burst into tears.

CHAPTER TWENTY ONE

Emily didn't know what to do with herself, who to speak to or where to turn. She could hear the murmuring of her guests in the living room as she passed and hoped that none had heard anything of the scene that had just unfolded. From the kitchen came the sounds of Serena and Parker chatting and the clinking of glasses and crockery as they tidied up for the day. Though Emily thought of Serena as a good friend, she couldn't quite bring herself to reveal what had happened, to admit that her world was coming crashing down around her. For the first time since she'd opened the B&B's doors, Emily craved solitude.

Emily was suddenly compelled to ascend the staircase and head up through the second floor and onto the third in search of the widow's walk from her memory. She wanted to feel close to her dad, to feel that same sense of protection she had when they'd watched the fireworks there together all those years ago. She raced up the stairs like a tornado.

Blinded by her tears, she followed the corridor down to the end. But when she got there, she found that there was only wallpaper, no door like in her memory of the widow's walk. Frustration took hold of Emily's rationality. She reached out, fingernails bared, and scraped them down the wallpaper, letting all her anger and rage out. The wallpaper came away beneath her fingernails, leaving streaks like claw marks.

That's when Emily realized what was behind the wallpaper. Not bricks or plaster, but wood. She began to rip the paper more feverishly, tearing great strips off and throwing them in the air, peeling it away until she was facing a small door. Another concealed door, like the one that led to the ballroom.

Emily understood now why the memory of the widow's walk had faded so completely from her memory. Her father had erased the proof of its existence. But why? What on earth had compelled her father to hide parts of the house?

Emily grabbed the small brass handle and twisted. Despite having been hidden away for so many years, the handle turned and the door creaked open.

The spiral staircase behind the door was just the same as in Emily's memory: dark and winding. She stepped inside carefully, as though walking into a museum. On the wall she saw the distinctive print of a child's hand and held her own up to it, wondering if it was indeed her own handprint from the past. Then she ascended the stairs slowly, feeling the breeze coming down from the top.

Finally, she reached the door at the top and shoved it open with her shoulder. All at once, Emily found herself amongst the tops of the evergreens. Through the branches she could see lights twinkling in the town and the masts of boats in the harbor. She was on the roof, around the side of the house that was only visible from the street but which was obscured by the evergreens. The widow's walk had been completely concealed from view, almost as if it had been erased from history. Emily wondered if this would be another piece of the puzzle that was the mystery of her father's disappearance.

CHAPTER TWENTY TWO

"What can I get you two ladies?" Gordon asked, leaning across the bar to where Cynthia and Emily stood.

"I think it's a Tom Collins kind of a night, don't you?" Cynthia said, nudging Emily.

Emily grunted her agreement and Gordon went off to fix the cocktails. As soon as he was gone, Cynthia motioned to one of the bar stools.

"You look like you need to sit down, dear," she said. "And then maybe you should explain why you decided you wanted to hit the town with an old eccentric like me!"

It was true that Cynthia Jones was not Emily's first choice of drinking companion. But she'd needed to get out of the house, and she'd needed someone to confide in, another woman to speak to openly about her troubles. Amy and Jayne lived miles away in New York, Serena was busy at the inn, Vanessa hadn't had enough energy to spend a night on the tiles since Katy was born, Sunita always came in a pair with Raj, and Karen was bound to be tucked up in bed early on a weeknight in order to get up ludicrously early to bake fresh bread for the store. So Cynthia's number had been the one that Emily found herself dialing after she'd climbed back down from the widow's walk. They'd met at Gordon's Bar down by the harborside, Emily still in her date night attire, Cynthia in a bright yellow skater dress and lime green cardigan.

Emily pulled up a stool and sank heavily down onto it.

"It's Daniel," she said with a sigh.

"Oh?" Cynthia replied, raising an eyebrow.

Just then, Gordon placed the two cocktails in front of the women. Emily grabbed hers immediately and took a swig.

"What's happened?" Cynthia prompted. "Did you have a fight?"

Emily shook her head. "More like, he has another girlfriend. And they have a kid together," she added with sarcastic enthusiasm.

Cynthia's mouth dropped open. "How much of that was a joke?" she stammered.

"None of it, unfortunately," Emily replied.

"I just don't believe it," Cynthia muttered. "He was hiding it from you?"

Emily shrugged. "I don't know," she admitted. "He said he didn't know about the kid. And the woman had a southern accent so I think she was his girlfriend when he lived in Tennessee, which would be quite a distance to travel to cheat on someone." She swallowed hard, the word *cheat* sticking in her throat. "I just don't know what to think."

Cynthia patted her arm. "If you feel like you need some space, you can stay at my place."

Emily smiled, comforted somewhat by Cynthia's kind words, but knowing she wouldn't be able to take up the offer. She had guests to look after. A B&B to run. Not to mention that staying with Cynthia and her teenage son wasn't what she wanted. She wanted to go home to her B&B, to the place she loved so dearly, and have it not be tarnished by the awful events of that evening. She wanted to go back in time, to the point when she was happy, to that moment before she'd bumped into Sheila on her porch.

"Oh," Cynthia said suddenly, in such a way that made Emily jerk up out of her slumped position.

She glanced behind her toward where Cynthia's attention was focused and saw Daniel standing in the door of the bar, looking around frantically. The second their eyes met, relief washed over his face.

"Emily," he gasped, rushing over. "I've been looking for you everywhere."

"Didn't that make you think that maybe I didn't want to be found?" Emily spat back.

Daniel seemed crushed. His whole expression was etched with pain. "Can you please just let me tell you my side of the story?"

Emily wanted him to go away. She'd been hurt by men in the past. Daniel was just another to add to a growing list of jerks she'd had the bad taste of getting attached to. But something made her relent.

"Fine," Emily said coldly, folding her arms. "Explain."

Daniel took a seat beside her. Cynthia slid away, Tom Collins in hand, leaving the two of them to talk alone.

"Sheila was a girlfriend from when I lived in Tennessee," Daniel began.

"The one with the husband?"

He nodded. "But we haven't been together for six years. She's not my girlfriend."

"Then why did you look so terrified when you saw her?" Emily asked coolly. "Or was that just because you knew she was about to give away your secret?"

Daniel rubbed his neck. "I had no idea about the child. You have to believe me."

Emily shot him a withering look.

"Please," he added. "I'm as shocked as you are. Sheila and I dated six years ago and then we broke up and I left. I had no idea at all that she'd been pregnant. She never told me."

"Did you give her a chance to tell you?" Emily asked. "Or did you just walk out on her one day?"

Daniel seemed to deflate at her words. Emily knew she'd hit the nail on the head.

"Look, I'm not proud of the things I've done in my past," Daniel said. "You know that. I've told you about some of that stuff before. But this is totally off the charts. I had no idea. None at all. It's not my fault she never told me. I mean, how was I supposed to know? I'm more upset than you, actually. Think about me for a second. That is my daughter. I have a daughter in the world, and I was never given the chance to raise her. How do you think that makes me feel?"

Emily could hear the anguish in his voice, and she could tell he was being sincere. She took a deep breath.

"Okay. You've said your piece. Now can I get back to my drinks with Cynthia? I'll… I guess I'll call you when I've got my head around all of this."

Daniel looked even more perturbed. "That's the thing," he began. From the tone of his voice, Emily could already tell that she did not like where this was heading. "There might not be time."

She frowned in confusion.

Daniel continued. "Sheila's not stable. She's left the kid—my daughter—with some uncle." He produced something from his pocket and slid it across the table to Emily. Emily looked down at the crumpled photograph on the table and the sweet girl beaming up at her. Her resemblance to Daniel was irrefutable. "I can't let that kid's life be ruined," he finished.

Emily looked from the picture up to Daniel. "What do you mean?"

Daniel paused for a long time. "I have to go. With Sheila. Back to Tennessee."

Emily stared at him, almost unable to comprehend or process the words he was telling her. This was her worst nightmare come true. Daniel was abandoning her. Not for another woman like she'd always feared, but for a daughter she'd never for a second imagined existed.

"Why?" she stammered.

"I need to help Sheila get back on her feet," Daniel said. "Help her find a proper apartment. See if I can persuade her into some kind of treatment program. If I don't then I'll be leaving my daughter with the same kind of chaotic upbringing I had. I can't do that to her."

"How long will that take?"

"I don't know," Daniel said with a heavy sigh. "A week. Two. Maybe more. All I can promise is that I will come back. No later than the end of the summer, once I've had the kid enrolled in a decent school."

Emily swallowed hard as she imagined the next six long weeks without Daniel by her side. She'd been so foolish to imagine spending the summer with him, to have daydreamed about more dates on the beach and lazy mornings in bed. Now it might not even happen.

Tears began to fall from Emily's eyes. "What if you don't want to come back? Once you've found her a school to go to and a place she calls home, what if you fall into a happy family routine?"

Daniel shook his head and grasped her hands. "It won't be like that. I promise. I'm coming back to you. I just need to meet her. Spend some time with her. Help bring some stability back into her life. But I promise you I'll be back before summer is over."

Emily's tears fell now in torrents. "You can't," she said as the realization hit her with a great wave of grief. "You can't let that poor girl think her dad is back, then up and leave her again."

Emily couldn't help but be reminded of her own bitter experiences, of her own father walking out on her. "You can't do that to her," she added, anger making her voice rise.

Emily knew that Daniel was just trying to do the right thing, but either way, someone would get hurt: the woman he never returned to or the little girl he left behind. She might love Daniel with all her heart, but she would never be selfish enough to rip a father from his daughter.

"If you leave her," she said through her bitter tears, "you won't be the sort of man I want to be with anyway."

Daniel's mouth dropped open as the understanding of what Emily was really saying hit him. "Are you giving me an ultimatum? You or her?"

Emily shook her head. "I'm giving you an out, Daniel. I'm giving you a free pass. I don't want you to choose between us. I want you to choose her. You have to. There's no other option."

Daniel gazed at her for a moment longer, hesitating as though trying to say something. Emily couldn't look at him anymore. She turned her gaze to the surface of the table. The next time she looked up, Daniel was gone.

CHAPTER TWENTY THREE

Sunlight blinding her vision, Emily watched from her bedroom window as Daniel packed up his truck early the next morning. She couldn't help but feel guilty about the angry words she'd fired at him in the bar. In reality, she didn't want him to leave, she wanted to be selfish, to put her needs first. But there was a part of her—the very real and demanding damaged child inside of her—that wanted Daniel to do the right thing for this innocent girl. It wasn't the girl's fault, just as it had not been Emily's. She would not wish the experience of losing a father on anyone, not even her worst enemy.

Just then, a soft knock came on the door. Emily let the curtain fall shut on Daniel then went over and unlocked it. She found Serena standing there. Sounds of merriment floated up from the reunion party downstairs.

"They're checking out now," Serena said. "Gus wanted to thank you personally."

Emily quickly wiped her tears away.

"Coming," she said, rearranging her expression into her game face.

Out in the hall, the brightness and warmth of the B&B encompassed her. She could hear all the joyous conversations floating up the staircase. In spite of everything that was going on, Emily felt a tug of a smile at her lips, knowing she'd done a good job, that at the very least she'd succeeded at this.

She followed Serena downstairs to where the reunion guests were congregating in the hall with their suitcases, waiting for cabs. Gus waved her over.

"Emily, I wanted to thank you for saving our weekend. We wouldn't have had anywhere near as good a time if it weren't for you. I think we'll book next year too, if that's okay with you?"

Emily faltered. Next year? It hit her then that perhaps there wouldn't be a next year. Not just because the B&B was struggling to stay afloat, but because she wasn't sure if she'd want to be here anymore, in this place, without Daniel.

Serena must have noticed that Emily was distracted. She walked over and said, "We haven't got our calendar ready for next year, but as soon as we do we'll be in touch."

Gus nodded and seemed satisfied with the answer. "I look forward to it."

Georgia Walters came up to Emily. "I've passed your details onto my granddaughter. She's getting married at the end of August and she has thirty guests that need somewhere to stay."

Emily quickly calculated in her head whether she'd be able to get the next ten rooms ready within six weeks and reasoned that if she could fix up the entire third floor in twenty-four hours, she could fix up ten more rooms in six weeks.

"That's great," Emily said. She knew she should be relieved that she wouldn't have to wait too long for her next source of income, but she felt flat and robotic. Numb.

From across the corridor, she saw Serena give her a thumbs-up. Her young friend's optimism and enthusiasm helped bolster Emily, though only a little.

Just then, Emily heard the cabs coming up the drive and went to the door to show the guests out. Once there, she noticed that Daniel's truck was gone and the carriage house was in darkness.

Feeling dazed, she said goodbye to each of the guests by name. But despite their compliments, cheek kisses, and handshakes, she felt unable to truly connect with any of them. She felt like she had been hollowed out. She was empty, with nothing to give. All she could do was play the part of the happy hostess and hope that no one noticed.

Of course, her routine didn't wash with her dear friend.

Serena came up beside her and waved off the guests with her. "What's going on?" she asked out the corner of her mouth.

"I can't tell you right now," Emily replied. "Because if I say it, I'll cry."

They kept waving as the cabs disappeared out of sight. But no sooner had they gone than another car began to drive up the path. Emily frowned, unsure as to who it could be. She watched as an elderly woman got out of the car and waved.

"Were you expecting another guest?" Serena asked.

Emily shook her head.

The woman walked slowly up toward them. "Hi. Emily?" she said, holding her hand out to shake. "I'm Anne Maroney."

Suddenly it clicked into place. The diamond lady! Emily had completely forgotten about the appointment she'd booked before the reunion party took over every second of available brain power she possessed.

"Serena, would you mind making some coffee?"

"No problem," Serena said.

Emily could tell she still desperately wanted to know what was going on but it was just going to have to wait. Just like all the tears

Emily was desperate to shed, she was going to have put them to the side for a moment longer.

"Would you mind having the meeting on the porch?" Emily said. "I'm afraid I've just had a function and the B&B was fully booked. It's not looking its best."

"The grounds are quite splendid," Anne said, "so I'll be very happy to sit out here."

"Wonderful. Take a seat. I'll go fetch the diamond."

Emily rushed upstairs into her bedroom and took the mahogany box out of her drawer. Then she went downstairs, bumping into Serena with the coffee in the hall.

"Emily," Serena said. "What's going on?"

Emily shook her head. "I can't talk about it right now, okay? I just have to get through this meeting with the diamond buyer, then I'll tell you everything."

Emily and Serena went outside and sat on the porch bench next to Anne. Emily placed the box on the table and Anne opened it up. She gasped when she saw the diamond.

"Gosh, this is much larger than what you told me on the phone."

"Is it?" Emily said. "I just read what was on the certificate."

She placed the certificate on the table, careful not to expose the lighthouse on the other side; the last thing she could handle right now were questions about her dad.

Anne peered at the certificate and then shook her head. "This certificate isn't the correct one for this diamond."

Emily immediately tensed. She'd already spent the money from the diamond sale on the roofing. The certificate couldn't be inaccurate!

"It's not a forgery or something, is it?" Emily said, biting her lip.

"Not as far as I can tell," Anne said, peering at it more closely. "It's just for a different diamond." She looked up at Emily. "The diamond you described sounded like it was for a wedding ring."

Emily wondered then if her father had accidentally stored the wrong certificate with the wrong diamond, had mixed up the certificates by accident. Or maybe he had stored the piece of paper only for the drawing on the back and it had been a coincidence that he'd stored it with a diamond at all. Thoughts swirled through Emily's mind. At the forefront was the terrible realization that she might not be getting any money from the diamond after all.

"So?" she said, chewing her lip. "Is it worth anything?"

Anne's eyes widened. "Worth anything? Emily, this is a thirty-thousand-dollar diamond!"

Next to Emily, Serena became very still. Emily too felt like she'd been turned into a statue.

"I'm sorry?" she stammered.

Anne nodded. "It's utterly flawless. A real gem. Whoever bought must have been a gemologist. Either that or they just had an eye for this sort of thing. Of course, it could have been fluke or an heirloom passed down through the generations. Do you know?"

Emily shook her head, too astonished to speak. She couldn't believe what she was hearing. After all the bad luck she'd suffered through, to find out the diamond was worth such a huge sum of money was like a dream come true.

"Well," Anne added, "I'm honestly thrilled to even be here. That is, if you'll still let me buy it from you?"

"Of course I will!" Emily exclaimed, elated.

As Anne pulled out her checkbook, Serena touched Emily's hand.

"Don't you want to get a second appraisal done?" she said under her breath. "Now that you know how much it's worth?"

Emily shook her head. She trusted Anne fully. Plus, she was making three times the amount she was expecting and that was more important to her than getting the best deal.

Anne handed her a check. $30,000. Emily was so thrilled.

"Thank you so much," she said, shaking Anne's hand.

"And thank you!" Anne replied.

Anne left in her car with the diamond, and Emily breathed a sigh of relief to know she was finally, at long last, back in the black.

"So can you please tell me what's going on now?" Serena asked, finally catching up with her.

Emily looked at her and said simply, "He's gone. Daniel."

"What?" Serena cried. "What do you mean gone? Gone where?"

"To Tennessee. To his daughter." Emily swished off inside the B&B, leaving Serena floundering on the doorstep.

"I don't understand," Serena said, following her inside. "He has a daughter?"

"Yup," Emily said, as she began tidying up the hallway after the guests.

Serena gasped. "But how?"

"I'm sure you don't need a biology lesson from me," Emily said, still busying her hands by organizing the hallway.

Serena rushed up to Emily and grabbed her hands, stopping her from fussing. "Emily, stop for a second, will you?"

Emily finally met her eyes.

"What are you going to do?" Serena asked.

Emily gritted her teeth with determination. "The only thing I can do," she said. "Prepare my B&B for thirty wedding guests."

CHAPTER TWENTY FOUR

SIX WEEKS LATER

· Emily could not remember a summer that had passed by so quickly and left her feeling so bitterly cold. Life without Daniel seemed dull and monotonous. Every morning she awoke to yet another glorious summer day—the sunshine so incongruous with her dark mood—then went over to the balcony and looked across the lawns to the carriage house. Every morning she was greeted with the same sight: the empty driveway, the carriage house in darkness. It was as if the summer was mocking her, its brightness making the shadows of the empty carriage house even starker and more foreboding.

As the summer sifted away, Emily threw herself into work, trying to keep herself occupied and her mind distracted by anything other than Daniel. She'd had the last ten rooms of the B&B done up, ready for the thirty wedding guests staying at the end of August, and had hosted a delightful Canadian family gathering, Anne Maroney and her partner, the lady from the department store in Maine, and some Japanese tourists visiting for the summer. She'd held Sunday brunches for the locals, ball game tournaments for the kids on the lawns, and even some evening outdoor films.

But every evening she went to bed with the same feeling of loneliness. It was a loneliness far worse even than the first nights she'd spent here in the dusty dilapidated house, mourning the loss of her New York life, her job, and the last seven years she'd spent with Ben. This time, Emily realized she'd lost something she loved more than all of those things, something that meant more to her than her job, apartment, and ex-boyfriend ever had. If it hadn't been for the wedding party booking keeping her here, Emily was certain she'd have packed everything in and run away by now.

Emily walked through the B&B admiring the beautiful decorations. She and Serena had spent many hours putting up the crisp white ribbons for the wedding party taking place tomorrow, and the house had transformed into a palace. On one wall, Serena had crafted a beautiful family tree out of wood. It had curling branches and the names of everyone in the wedding party's families on each of the leaves.

Emily tried not to think of the significance of the date—the last day of August—but she couldn't help it. She'd been missing Daniel so desperately it was impossible not to count down the days. But if he came back to her like he promised, it would mean he'd abandoned his daughter, and in doing so had become a man that Emily could no longer love. It would be bittersweet.

Just then the doorbell rang and Emily's heart leaped into her throat. She reminded herself that Daniel wouldn't ring the doorbell, he'd just waltz right into the house. She calmed her fluttering heartbeat and opened the door.

In front of her was a stack of pearly white chairs.

"Chair delivery," a bored voice said from behind. "Where do you want them all?"

Emily pulled the door wide open. "They're going in the ballroom," she said.

"Ballroom?" the voice replied as the chairs began to rotate on their trolley. Finally the delivery man was revealed, a thin guy with a birdlike appearance.

"Yes, this way."

Emily showed him to the ballroom, where the indoor part of the party was to take place.

"Whoazer," the delivery man said as he wheeled the stack into place on his trolley. "This is incredible!"

On such a bright day, the Tiffany glass was refracting tiny rainbows all over the room. It looked magical. Emily couldn't help but think, painfully, of the time when she and Daniel had been in this room, talking enthusiastically about the possibility of using it as a wedding venue. Now that dream had become a reality, but Daniel was not here to share it with her. She felt his absence too keenly, like a hole in her heart. And no matter how much she threw herself into work, that yearning never seemed to diminish.

Emily helped put the chairs into their positions and saw the delivery guy out. Just then her phone started to ring and she saw that it was Karen calling her.

"Emily," Karen said a little breathlessly. "I've finally done it."

"Done what?" Emily asked.

"I've got the meeting. For your sign."

"Oh!" Emily exclaimed. It had almost slipped her mind that Karen had agreed so many weeks ago to help sort out the ongoing dispute about her sign. Trevor had done such a thorough job at blocking the application process that Emily had just become accustomed to all the setbacks, to the dry voicemails Marcella would leave her explaining there'd been a change of plans *due to a new formal complaint being submitted*. And what with Daniel's absence she hadn't really noticed the absence of the sign also.

"It's tomorrow," Karen continued.

"Tomorrow!" Emily exclaimed. It was just her luck that the meeting would be scheduled for a Saturday, on the one day she already had a ton of work to do. "What time?"

"Nine a.m.," Karen said. "I know it's short notice. Can you make it?"

"Of course," Emily replied, though she felt a little exasperated. At least it didn't clash with the wedding party. She'd be able to do both. And anyway, she could do with having as many distractions tomorrow as possible.

"Great," Karen said, sounding more excited than Emily felt. "We're going to get your sign back. I promise. I'll see you then."

She hung up and Emily glanced at the receiver in her hand, feeling somewhat deflated and harried. She wondered whether Trevor had engineered it so the meeting would fall at such an awkward time, ensuring that she'd have the least amount of preparation time as possible. She didn't put anything past him.

Emily got back to the work in hand. She glanced through the long list of preparations. Everything had to be perfect for tomorrow. She knew that if it had been her wedding taking place, she'd want everything perfect.

There were more deliveries coming tomorrow—the cake, the ice sculpture, and all the flowers—but for today, everything that needed to be done had. And that meant she had a night off to prepare for the upcoming meeting.

Just then her cell phone rang. It was Amy. Emily answered it, relieved to have a friendly voice to speak to.

"I have a secret," Amy said the second Emily answered the phone.

"Okay…" Emily said, a little suspicious.

"I'll let Jayne explain," Amy said.

More confused than ever, Emily frowned as she listened to the sound of the cell being passed over. Then Jayne's voice came over the line.

"Guess what!" Jayne exclaimed.

"Can I have a clue?" Emily asked.

"Um, okay, hold on."

Emily heard the sound of a car horn tooting, then Amy's voice exclaiming, "Hey! Don't do that! We'll get pulled over!"

Jayne came back on the line. "Have you guessed yet?"

Emily rubbed her face with her hand. She was stressed and didn't have the time or energy for Jayne at the moment. "I don't know. You're in a car."

"Yes!" Jayne exclaimed. "And why might we be in a car?"

"Because you're going on a road trip," Emily said, still struggling to muster any kind of enthusiasm.

"And where might we be on a road trip to?" Jayne asked.

"I don't know," Emily said with a large sigh. "Philadelphia?"

"Nope," Jayne said. "Sunset Harbor!"

She squealed the last bit so loudly Emily almost dropped the phone. Then there was a long pause while Emily collected her thoughts.

"Oh." She tried to say it brightly, but her mind was frantic. She couldn't have Jayne and Amy over for the night! Not with the wedding and the meeting and everything that was going on with Daniel.

"You don't sound pleased," Jayne said, sounding deflated.

"It's not that," Emily said. "I love you girls, you know that. I'm just really swamped at the moment."

"Oh, come on," Jayne said in her eye-rolling voice. "You're rattling around in that big house all by yourself. You need some company."

It was true that Emily could do with some human company—Mogsy and Rain were delightful but they weren't quite the same. She just wished they'd been able to get their act together and visit her some time in the last six weeks when she'd had time a-plenty and desperately needed some shoulders to cry on! It just felt so typical, Emily thought, for everything to happen at once.

"Where are you now?" Emily asked. She hoped they hadn't traveled too far, that she could convince them that tonight just wasn't a good idea.

"We're on the coast," Jayne said. "Ames, where are we?"

"Portland," she heard Amy call.

Emily sighed loudly. They were almost there.

"Well, I don't have much choice in the matter now really, do I?" Emily said. "You'll just have to accept that I'm going to be busy. How long are you staying?"

"Just overnight," Jayne said. "Jeez, could you sound any less pleased about this?"

Emily's patience was waning. She wanted to snap at Jayne, to offload all the worries and concerns that were swimming in her mind, but she knew it wasn't her friend's fault. If anything, having Amy and Jayne here could make things a little easier. It would be good for her to be distracted at this time.

"I'm sorry," she said eventually. "I'm just in a bit of a weird place at the moment. I'll tell you all about it when you get here."

"Great," Jayne said. "We won't be long. I think it's an hour or so. Ames is nodding her head. So an hour. See you then."

She hung up before Emily had a chance to say more.

*

As the hour wore on, Emily felt better and better about seeing Amy and Jayne. She recognized the sensation inside of her and realized she was feeling excitement for the first time in a long time. As reluctant as she was about how busy she was going to be, she realized that she needed their company more now than anyone else's. She loved her Sunset Harbor friends but they were far too close to the situation. Her New York friends were removed enough for it not to overshadow everything. Emily was getting sick of all the sympathetic and forlorn faces everyone kept giving her, like she was a wounded animal or something.

At midday, Emily heard the sound of a car being noisily driven up the gravel path. She rushed to the door and saw her two friends leaping out of their car in high spirits. Jayne was dressed to the nines, her black hair glossy, her fingernails painted crimson. As Emily trotted down the porch steps to greet them she noticed the curtains flicker in Trevor Mann's top room, the one she presumed he used to secretly spy on her every time she made too much noise for his liking. He was probably up there writing his arguments for their meeting tomorrow.

"Em!" Jayne cried, practically throwing herself at Emily. The smell of her perfume hit Emily like a wave.

Emily accepted her hug greedily. It had been too long since she'd been embraced. She felt herself well up at that thought.

Jayne let go and then Amy approached. They hadn't seen each other since the last town meeting when Mayor Hansen had granted Emily the permit to run the B&B. Though they'd spoken a little bit since, Emily wasn't entirely sure where they stood at the moment.

"You cut your hair," Emily said as a way of breaking the ice.

Amy nodded, her new chin-length bob swaying as she did. Then she burst into a smile and pulled her old friend into a bear hug. "I've missed you, Emily."

"I've missed you too," Emily replied, breathing a sigh of relief.

"Now," Jayne said, addressing Amy, "there's nothing to do here so we just sit on the porch and get drunk. Isn't that right, Em?"

Emily shrugged. "Pretty much. But you have to be careful. There's a wedding party here tomorrow evening. Don't snoop. Or break anything."

Jayne gave her a look. "What makes you think we'll break anything?"

Amy was more diplomatic. "We're just here for one girly night in with our best friend in her ridiculously gorgeous house."

Emily smiled at that. "I supposed I'd better make a pitcher of mojitos then."

Her two friends followed her into the kitchen, where Rain and Mogsy began yapping and running about excitedly. Jayne and Amy were thrilled to meet them and bestowed hugs and kisses on them.

"Oh my God," Jayne squealed. "I wish I had an apartment big enough for a puppy."

"You'd never be able to have one," Amy contested. "You work too much. Not that you don't work, Emily," she added hurriedly, "I just mean you have to be home all the time if you want pet dogs."

Emily nodded. "I definitely didn't plan on it," she said, "but it's pretty neat having them around. They stop me getting lonely." She paused as soon as she'd said the words and swallowed. She hadn't been planning on diving straight into the Daniel-abandoning-her situation—that was a two-glasses-of-mojitos-later kind of topic.

Luckily, neither of her friends seemed to notice the slip-up.

"Ames, why don't you tell Emily all about your new boyfriend?" Jayne said, her eyes sparkling mischievously.

"Boyfriend?" Emily asked, her eyes widening with astonishment. Amy was far too sensible for boyfriends. She only ever dated and none of her relationships ever lasted particularly long. For it to have gotten to boyfriend status meant it was pretty serious.

Amy shifted uncomfortably. Then she brought her wallet out of her purse and handed Emily a picture. It was of her and an impossibly handsome man arm in arm on a sunny beach.

"Where is this?" Emily exclaimed.

"Hawaii," Amy replied, blushing. "He took us for our three-month anniversary."

Emily couldn't believe it. She kept staring at the photo, at Amy's face in it. Her friend looked happier than she'd ever seen her.

"What's his name?" she stammered.

"Frasier," Amy said. "He's thirty-eight."

"And totally loaded!" Jayne interjected. "He works in investment banking but it's also in the family, you know?"

Emily looked back down at the happy, healthy Frasier, with his perfectly straight white teeth and shiny hair. He and Amy looked like Mr. and Mrs. Perfect. Emily couldn't help but feel a pang of jealousy. Had she made a huge mistake getting so wrapped up in Daniel? They both had such flawed histories and their relationship had already been through so many rocky patches. Maybe she was being stupid for wanting to settle with him, for waiting for him. What if there was a Mr. Perfect waiting to whisk her off to Hawaii?

"Why didn't you tell me you had a boyfriend?" Emily asked.

Amy shrugged. "I guess I got a bit wrapped up in it all. I mean you of all people know what it's like when you get into a great relationship!"

Emily felt her emotions hit her like a wave of grief. Before she could even stop herself, she began to cry.

Amy and Jayne exchanged a worried glance.

"What's wrong?" Amy asked gently. "Has something happened with Daniel?"

"He's gone," Emily managed to squeeze out between her sobs.

"Gone?" Amy repeated, handing Emily a tissue. "Where?"

Emily dabbed at her tears. "He's gone to Tennessee to be with his daughter."

"He has a daughter?" Jayne spat, her mouth wide open with astonishment. "And let me guess, he didn't have the good grace to tell you about her?"

Emily shook her head. "He didn't know she existed," she mumbled, not quite able to meet her friends' eyes. She shouldn't be making excuses for him.

"Oh, babe," Amy said. "When did all this happen?"

"Six weeks ago," Emily admitted. "I was too embarrassed to tell you."

"I'm not surprised," Jayne replied. "I mean I'd be mortified if that happened to me. Like, beyond embarrassed."

Amy glared at her.

"But that's just me," Jayne said, floundering, "You have no reason to be embarrassed. It's Daniel who's been a huge jerk. What kind of idiot gets his girlfriend pregnant then doesn't even stick around to meet the kid?"

"Has he been in contact?" Amy asked.

Emily could feel the blush of shame rising in her cheeks. She busied herself crushing ice. "No. He doesn't have a cell phone, though, so I wasn't expecting him to." She knew it sounded like a lame excuse, but it was Daniel's way, and something she'd accepted about him. "But he promised me he'd be back before the end of summer."

"He's cutting it a bit fine, don't you think?" Jayne said.

Emily nodded, her gaze still averted.

"You don't think he will?" Amy asked gently.

Emily shrugged. "I don't know. Even if he does come back, nothing can be the same again, can it? He's a father now. That changes everything. If he comes back to me that means he chose me over his daughter and that makes him the kind of man I don't want to be with. Either way I lose."

Amy rubbed her arm kindly.

Jayne was a little more blunt than Amy about the whole thing. "Well, he was just your Ben rebound, wasn't he? I mean he was a lumberjack. You can't have had that much to talk about."

"We had plenty to talk about," Emily rebuked her.

"It's okay, Em," Jayne added. "Just being with a guy because he's good between the sheets is fine. We've all done it."

"I loved him," Emily protested.

"Loved?" Amy said, interjecting. "As in past tense? As in not anymore?"

"As in, I don't know," Emily said with a heavy sigh. "It's all too confusing. I guess I'll just have to wait and see what happens."

Emily tried to ignore the doubtful look her friends shared.

"So, how many people are coming to the wedding party tomorrow?" Amy asked in what Emily recognized as an attempt to steer the conversation away from the painful topic.

"Thirty," Emily said. "The whole B&B is booked up."

"That's pretty neat," Amy replied. "You've been getting lots of bookings then?"

Emily finished making the mojitos and they went out to drink them on the porch. "Actually, not a huge amount. I had a fiftieth high school reunion party over the long Fourth of July weekend. There were twenty of those guys. Surprisingly rowdy for seventy-year-olds. Then I've had a few guests here and there but nothing much until this."

"Enough to make ends meet?" Jayne asked.

Emily chewed her lip. "Not really. I mean there's so much to spend in the first place. Just getting the house to a livable standard has been expensive enough, not to mention the roof leaking and ruining a ton of antiques. Then there's staff costs and, well, anyway, you get the picture."

Amy and Jayne exchanged a glance then. Emily could tell there was something they were holding back.

"What is it?" she asked.

It was Amy who spoke. "It's my candle company," she said. "It's going really well at the moment. I'm expanding. I have an office in an actual building rather than just my apartment." She smiled shyly.

Emily wasn't sure why Amy had been so reticent to mention her success. Maybe she was worried that it was insensitive territory to tread considering that Emily's own business was always teetering on the brink of ruin.

"That's great," Emily said. "I'm really happy for you."

"Well," Amy continued, and Emily realized she wasn't done yet. There was more to come. "I was really hoping you'd be interested in coming home to be the marketing manager. Jayne's agreed to head the sales team. I don't know if there's anyone else I trust more in the world to be part of the senior management team than you two."

Emily was shocked. She'd worked in marketing for years when she was in New York but had never quite reached the place in her career she'd wanted to. She'd always dreamed of climbing up the ranks but it had never really happened that way. She'd always blamed herself, though after moving to Sunset Harbor she'd wondered whether it was actually Ben holding her back more than just a general lack of confidence in herself.

But now everything was different. She was different. The thought of working in New York again filled her with dread. Just the commute was enough to put her off.

"I don't know," she said. "I have this place to think of."

"You mean you have Daniel to think of?" Jayne said, raising an eyebrow.

"I can't just up and walk away," Emily protested.

"Why not?" Jayne challenged her. "He did."

"This isn't about Daniel," Emily said, her tone becoming sharper. "This is about my life. My business. About who I'm becoming, or at least who I want to become."

Jayne shook her head. It was starting to get a little bit heated. "You want to host old folks' parties at a failing B&B in a quiet, boring town? Really? That's what you want?"

Emily's jaw slackened. She couldn't believe how cutting Jayne was being. Amy, ever the peacemaker, stepped in.

"You don't need to make a decision anytime soon," she said, gently. "I think what Jayne is trying to express is that we miss you and want you home."

Emily huffed. "She has a funny way of saying it," she mumbled.

But she knew Amy was right. Jayne just wanted her back in New York, back where they believed she belonged. She wondered if she did still belong there after all. If maybe life would be easier if she just packed this all in and went back with them. She could go on Sunday as soon as the wedding party guests had checked out, just up and leave without telling anyone, without giving a forwarding address. If she left her cell phone, no one would even be able to contact her or track her down. But if she did, she'd always be left wondering whether Daniel came back to her or not, whether there was any chance of a future for them.

"You've had a great few months here," Amy said. "But the summer's almost over. You should come back."

Emily couldn't meet either of their eyes. "I'll think about it," she said.

And to her surprise, she realized that she meant it. She really was considering returning to New York. As much as she didn't want it to be about Daniel, she knew that it was. It was the last weekend of August. If Daniel didn't show up by the end of Sunday, then she'd know once and for all that it was over between them, that he'd chosen the happy family life in Tennessee just like she feared he would. And if there was no Daniel in Sunset Harbor anymore, maybe there'd be no reason for Emily herself to remain here either.

CHAPTER TWENTY FIVE

Up in her room, Emily pulled her suitcase out of the back of the cupboard. Most of her personal possessions were now packed away, just in case she needed to make a quick exit.

Her room was a mess at the moment. After the last few rooms on the third floor had been renovated, she'd had nowhere to store her dad's boxes so she'd temporarily dumped them in here; it wasn't like she had to keep her room tidy for anyone anymore. The boxes had originally been in the throw-out category, but after all the talk of Barcelona she wondered whether there'd been any evidence that she'd overlooked at first.

She sat down now and began to rummage through one of the boxes. There was nothing of interest in it, though she did find another sketch of the lighthouse her father had been so obsessed with. This one had been done in oil. She'd found so many now that she'd begun to wonder if the artist was in fact her father. Of course, she'd never seen him show any interest in making art, but then she'd also never heard him speak about Barcelona, so why not? Her mind came up with all kinds of ludicrous ideas. Like maybe he had a secret double life as a creative, frequenting art galleries by night while smoking cigars and wearing a black beret. Or maybe the artist was his secret child—if Daniel could have one, why not her dad? Or maybe he had a lover. Anne Maroney had said the diamond certificate was for a wedding ring, after all, so maybe her father had committed bigamy with the artist. They were crazy, paranoid thoughts, but she was beginning to suspect anything, beginning to wonder if she even knew her dad at all.

As she sifted through the box of papers, Emily felt increasingly sad and confused. But there was also a sense of nostalgia that came to her too, nostalgia for the man she remembered her father to be.

Just then the bell rang. Emily's heart leaped into her throat. Could it be Daniel?

She ran over to the window, peering out through the net curtains to see if there were lights on in the carriage house or any sign of his truck in the driveway. Everything was in darkness. But she could make out the silhouette of a car parked up in the driveway. It was sleek and expensive looking, certainly not the sort of car Daniel would usually drive, but stranger things happened.

As quietly as she could, Emily rushed downstairs, making sure not to wake her two friends who were each sleeping in the grandest rooms on the second floor. Her heart was racing when she got to the door and flung it open.

When she saw who was standing there, her heart seemed to stop beating entirely. He was more handsome than she remembered, his dark hair styled neatly, his smile sparkling.

Standing on her doorstep was Ben.

CHAPTER TWENTY SIX

"Oh my God," Emily managed to say.

It had been almost a year since she'd walked out on him. It looked so wrong seeing him on her porch, like he just didn't belong there.

"Hello, Emily," Ben said. "Can I come in?"

Emily's mind was swirling with thoughts. Just a moment ago she'd thought Daniel had returned to her but now she was face to face with Ben, of all people. She didn't know what to think or say or do.

"How did you find me?" she stammered. "How did you know I was here?"

Ben gave an apologetic shrug. "From Jayne. But don't kill her," he added. "I knew she was coming to see you today and I made her tell me where you were staying."

Emily exhaled with frustration. Typical of Jayne to poke her nose into her business. She must have messaged Ben the address the second she'd found out that Daniel was gone! It was an eight-hour drive to Sunset Harbor from New York so the time would only make sense if she had. Emily could feel herself growing more and more angry. Thanks to Jayne, Daniel's absence stung even more keenly. She'd been hoping so much that it would be him on her doorstep that to be confronted with the ghost of her past instead was a double blow.

Emily rubbed her forehead, trying to push away the frown line that seemed permanently etched there. "What are you doing here, Ben?" she said in a great exhalation. "It's late and I have an early start tomorrow."

"I wanted to talk to you," Ben said. "That's all I've wanted to do. I understand why you left, but to never answer my calls? To never give me a chance to talk it through with you?"

Emily felt suddenly guilty. Walking out on Ben like that was inexcusable behavior. It was the sort of thing the old Emily did, but not something the new Emily would ever, ever do. She had changed so much since she'd left New York. Hurting someone in that way was no longer in her nature.

She moved back from the doorway. "You're right. You'd better come in."

Ben smiled and stepped into the corridor. Right away he whistled. "Wow. You did all this? It's incredible."

Right now, Emily needed the compliment. "Thanks. So do you want a drink or anything? Wine? Beer?"

Ben shook his head. "No, I'm driving. Unless you want to let me book one of your rooms?" He smiled sheepishly as if to show that he was just joking.

"I'll get you a juice instead," Emily said. "It's organic. And freshly squeezed."

Ben looked impressed as he followed Emily down the corridor toward the kitchen. She noticed as they went that he kept glancing around him in awe, almost as if he couldn't believe that she'd created something so beautiful. It made that familiar bubble of anger rise inside of her; Ben had never seen her potential, never nurtured her talent. No wonder he was so surprised now by what she'd achieved all on her own.

They went into the kitchen and Ben whistled his approval. Needing something to calm her nerves a little, Emily poured herself a wine. Then she got some juice from the fridge for Ben and they sat at the kitchen table together. Emily couldn't help thinking of Daniel, of the way they sat here together drinking coffee in the mornings. It felt like Ben had muscled in on Daniel's territory, as though he were occupying Daniel's vacant space. Emily became even more aware of how much she missed Daniel, how lonely she had become without him over the last few weeks.

"I've been thinking a lot," Ben said. "About our relationship and how it went wrong."

Emily raised an eyebrow. "You have?" She herself had done all of her thinking during the relationship. As soon as it was done, she'd wiped her hands clean of it all and thrown herself into the B&B with Daniel. "Not like you to spend much time thinking," she added wryly.

Ben rubbed his neck, suddenly awkward. "I know. But you were important to me, Emily, and... well, I took you for granted, didn't I? I let you become an afterthought. I never listened to what you wanted. The house was decorated in my style. We went to my favorite restaurants. We hung out with my friends and family. It was all about me."

"Oh," Emily said, a little surprised. She hadn't expected Ben to be so insightful. "Is there an apology coming next?"

Ben nodded. "Yes. I'm sorry. Truly. I was a jerk. And I didn't realize what I had until it was gone."

Emily sipped her wine. "It happens to the best of us. That's why there's a whole bunch of proverbs about it." She looked up and smiled. "But thanks. I appreciate hearing that. And I'm sorry too for the way I left. It was harsh. And rude. And totally unnecessary."

Ben nodded in acknowledgment of her apology. "I can't believe what you've achieved here," he said. "I'm amazed."

"Thanks," Emily said. "I can't take all the credit. I've had a lot of help."

Ben seemed to become more quiet. "You mean Daniel?"

"I really am going to kill Jayne," Emily muttered under her breath. Then to Ben she replied, "Amongst other people. I've made a lot of friends here."

"But Daniel was special, right?" Ben asked, a mournful expression on his face. "He was more than a friend. Jayne said you loved him."

Emily took a deep breath. "I did. Do. It's complicated."

"Doesn't seem too complicated if you ask me," Ben said. "He's not here. He should be. If he loved you he would be."

Emily's gaze dropped to the tabletop. Maybe Ben was right. If Daniel loved her he wouldn't have put her through all this pain and anguish. At the very least he would have called. But then again, she had been the one to end it, hadn't she? It had been her words about him no longer being a man she respected that had sealed the fate on their relationship.

"Like I am," Ben said, his words jerking her from her thoughts.

Her eyes snapped up. "I'm sorry. What did you say?"

"I'm here because I love you, Emily," Ben said.

She shook her head. "No, you don't."

"I do," he insisted. "I always have. That's why I've been calling. I should never have let you walk out of that restaurant. I should have realized what you meant to me. It was only after you were gone that I realized how much I love you."

"I'm a different person now," Emily said, still shaking her head, feeling her heart beat wildly in her chest. "It's been months. I've changed. How can you know?"

But Ben didn't respond. Because suddenly he was kneeling.

"What are you doing?" Emily stammered, her heart leaping into her throat.

Ben produced a small black box from his pocket and snapped open the lid. Sitting inside was a silver ring with a large, beautiful diamond. Thanks to all of Emily's diamond research she could tell right away that it was a very, very expensive one. She gasped.

"I should have done this years ago," Ben said. "Emily Mitchell, will you marry me?"

CHAPTER TWENTY SEVEN

As Emily stared at the glittering ring, Ben's words repeated in her mind. He loved her? He wanted to marry her? Once she would have given anything in the world to hear him say those words.

"This isn't happening," she gasped.

Ben smiled, his eyes wide, his expression dewy. "It is, Emily. Please forgive me. I'll be a better man for you. I'll be the husband I should always have been."

Emily could hardly breathe. Ben was offering her the stability and commitment she'd always craved. It felt like fate had struck again, that Ben had been sent to her now when she was feeling her most vulnerable and doubtful about Daniel and the future, when she was just starting to feel like packing everything in and leaving this place. Here was the man she'd spent seven years building a life with telling her that he would make all her dreams come true.

There was just one catch. He wasn't Daniel.

Finally, Emily shook her head. "I'm sorry, Ben. I can't marry you."

Ben looked up at her, stunned. "But I thought this was what you wanted."

"It was. Once. But not anymore. I'm sorry."

Ben snapped the lid of the box shut. He looked utterly crushed. Emily had never seen him so dejected.

"Is this because of Daniel?" he asked. "Because you love him more than you love me?"

Emily looked down into her lap, a whole host of emotions assaulting her. Part of her felt like she was making a terrible mistake for not taking Ben up on his offer, but another, stronger, part of her knew that she would be settling for second best if she did. Ben might have wealth and stability, but Daniel gave her companionship. The short few months she'd known Daniel had changed her life more than the seven years she'd been with Ben.

"I'm a different person now," Emily explained.

Ben's eyes glittered with tears. "No, you're not, Emily. You're the same person I fell in love with. I saw it in your eyes the second you saw me standing on your porch."

Emily tried to speak but Ben wasn't finished. He grabbed her hand and the words tumbled out of him passionately.

"We don't have to get married," he said quickly. "If that's moving too quickly for you we can take a step back, just go back to New York and spend some time together, the two of us. I'll do whatever it takes to make you see that I want this, that I love you. I'll move as slowly or as quickly as you want."

Emily took a deep breath. Seeing Ben like this was shaking her to the core. She'd never expected to see such an outpouring of emotion, such honesty and vulnerability from him. His passion for her seemed to suddenly eclipse what she'd felt from Daniel. She could never imagine him proposing to her like this; he was too measured and practical.

But still it was Daniel her mind kept returning to.

Suddenly Ben was standing. "I'm going to go and let you think about things, okay? If you want to marry me, just say the word. And if you ever want to come back to New York then my door is always open for you. I'll wait. For however long it takes."

Emily had completely lost her voice. She couldn't even manage to say no, to tell him waiting for her was pointless because her heart now belonged to another. All she could do was stand there dumbly as Ben pulled her into him for a farewell embrace, breathing in the familiar smell of his cologne.

"Think about it," he said finally.

Then he swirled out of the kitchen and was gone.

CHAPTER TWENTY EIGHT

The next morning, Emily woke early, her head a little muggy from the mojitos, and dressed. The town meeting had been scheduled for 9 a.m. Emily couldn't help but wonder whether it was a cruel trick of Marcella's to place it so early in the day, or whether there was some silly scheduling rule she was following.

She dressed smartly in one of her B&B hostess outfits, then went to the vanity mirror to put in her earrings. From here, she had a clear view out the window of the whole front grounds of the B&B, including Daniel's carriage house, which was tucked neatly behind some trees. There was no sign of Daniel's truck in the driveway.

Yet, she thought.

Once dressed, Emily went downstairs and brewed a pot of coffee, making enough for Amy and Jayne to have some once they awoke. She was still mad at Jayne for blabbing about everything to Ben, and her mind was still reeling from the whole encounter. Seeing Ben down on one knee was an image that would forever be burned into her mind. She'd dreamed of that image so many times, but the reality of it had been nothing like she expected. And nothing like what she wanted. It amazed her how much her priorities and needs had changed since coming to Sunset Harbor.

Emily finished her coffee, then quickly scribbled a note for her friends saying they could help themselves to anything from the fridge as long as it wasn't on a large silver platter. Parker had been working on some new recipes for crudités that he wanted to try out on the wedding party and had created five platters' worth of them.

Finally ready to face the zoning board, Emily put on her game face, marched to the front door, pulled it open, and slammed straight into someone.

Daniel, she thought instantly, her heart missing a beat.

But she was sorely disappointed when she drew back and saw not the longed-for Daniel standing on her doorstep, but the much-maligned Trevor.

"Trevor," Emily said in one long exhalation. "To what do I owe the displeasure?"

"I was just thinking we could save ourselves a journey," Trevor said in his usual arrogant, haughty tone.

"You want to carpool to the meeting?" Emily asked, raising an eyebrow.

"Actually," Trevor sneered, "I was thinking we could skip the town meeting altogether." When Emily gave him a bemused expression, he added, "If you let me buy the house off you we wouldn't need to have a pesky meeting at all."

Emily folded her arms, instantly understanding what Trevor's whole campaign about getting her sign removed had really been about. She should have realized it sooner, that Trevor would pull a stunt like this. It was never about the sign being a blight on his ocean view, or about him trying to close down the B&B because of the increased traffic outside his property. Trevor had just been trying to push her right up to the edge of her patience. His whole motive, since the moment she'd set foot in Sunset Harbor, was to get the property off of her. It must have killed him seeing it sit there empty for twenty-five years, and then when she'd shown up he'd come around and offered a paltry amount to take it off her hands. When she'd refused, he'd started his campaign. He must have been thinking that if he just kept on prodding, poking, and provoking, she'd eventually give in and realize it was all far more hassle than it was worth. He must have thought she'd just be looking for a quick profit from the place, not having expected her to be so determined to make it succeed and keep it in her family.

"That's not going to happen, Trevor," Emily said. "I'm not selling the house to you for a paltry fifty thousand dollars. Now could you please move out of my way?"

Trevor stood his ground. "Last time I made you an offer, the place was little more than a dilapidated shed. Now you've restored it and it's looking quite wonderful. So I'm upping my offer to match market value. I'll give you five hundred thousand for it. That's ten times the amount I offered last time. It could be the quickest and easiest sale in the history of real estate."

Emily raised an eyebrow. Hearing the sum was a shock. It would be a life-changing amount, more money than she'd ever had before. She could buy herself a cute little apartment and live comfortably off the rest for a few years at least. But more than the fact she didn't trust Trevor at all was the fact that he was the last person in the world she would want to see the precious home fall into the hands of. The house was worth more to her than money; it contained memories, memories she'd only just begun to unlock. There was no way she could give them up.

"Read my lips, Trevor," Emily said firmly. "NO."

She shoved past him then, her patience spent, and headed to her car.

"In which case," Trevor called after her, "I'll see you at the meeting. And I will block you getting that sign back. Just you wait and see!"

Emily got into her car, her anger overwhelming her. It felt like another cruel trick that fate was playing, trying to force her hand. It would be so easy to just sell the B&B, to leave Sunset Harbor and head back to her new job in New York without ever knowing whether Daniel returned or not. But that was the operative word, Emily thought. *Easy.* Easy was akin to escape, and that was something Emily didn't want to do anymore. She didn't want to be an escapologist like her father had been. When the going got tough, she didn't want to run away.

And so Emily drove to the town meeting, fuming all the way. If she could just hold onto her anger at Trevor then she wouldn't break down.

When she got to the town hall, she saw that it was packed with her friends from town—Birk and Bertha, Jason and Vanessa, Charles and Barbara, Raj and Sunita, Cynthia, Parker, and Serena. She hadn't expected to see them all here. In fact, she hadn't expected to see any of them here! It reminded her why she loved Sunset Harbor in the first place. The friends she'd made here were wonderful people, full of love and generosity. Would escaping to New York really be the easy option, when there was all this she'd be leaving behind?

The only person absent was Daniel. Emily's stomach tightened at the thought of him. She was doing a lousy job keeping him off her mind.

Karen came over and pulled Emily into a hug. "We've got this, sweetie. Don't worry about a thing."

Emily hugged her tightly. She'd always viewed Karen in a maternal kind of way and wondered if this was what it felt like to be loved by one's mother.

Mayor Hansen called the meeting to order. "We're here to discuss the permit for the sign at the Inn at Sunset Harbor," he said. "I'll start by passing the floor to Trevor Mann, who has raised... *several...* objections to the sign."

Trevor looked like a horrible toad as he took to the stage. Emily rolled her eyes. Of course he'd prepared a speech.

"The inn is on a quiet residential street. I am being constantly disturbed by noise and increased traffic, and the last thing I need is this unsightly sign!"

Emily shook her head as she listened to all of his prepared excuses, each and every one of them just a ruse to get her to sell him the property.

"Anything else?" Mayor Hansen said, his voice sounding completely weary.

"Yes, actually," Trevor added with a sneer. "I'm raising a legal challenge to the sign through the Litter Pollution Act."

"Litter?" Karen scoffed, leaping to her feet. "How on earth can you categorize it as litter?"

The crowd began to babble amongst each other and look from one to the other. Emily caught Karen's eye and she shot her a worried expression. She'd assured Emily that Trevor had exploited every last legal challenge he had, yet somehow he'd still managed to seek out a loophole and exploit it.

Marcella was on her feet immediately, her local government rule book in hand. "I believe Mr. Mann is referring to Article 19 of the Litter Pollution Act 1997," she stated. "That the council may block posters, banners, and signs at their discretion if such advertisement is considered to be litter."

Mayor Hansen sighed and rolled his eyes. "Right, and how long will it take Miss Mitchell to contest this legal loophole?"

Now it was Emily's turn to stand. "How about no time at all," she said. She reached in her purse and pulled out a form. "I believe this is the correct paperwork needed to declare that the sign is not on public property and thus not subject to the rules of the Litter Pollution Act 1997, which is primarily used to stop electoral candidates from placing banners outside of the election campaign window."

A hushed silence fell across the audience. Everyone seemed stunned that Emily had come so prepared. But she'd had six weeks of loneliness to prepare for every eventuality of this meeting and had expected Trevor to pull such a trick out of his bag.

Trevor looked furious. Marcella began leafing through her binder. Finally she looked up and said, "Emily is quite right. As long as the paperwork has been filled in correctly we can get it stamped by the mayor right now and her sign will be exempt from the Litter Pollution Act."

Emily folded her arms and smiled triumphantly at Trevor, whose face had gone bright red with fury.

Marcella rushed over and took the form from Emily and handed it to the mayor. He adjusted his glasses and cleared his throat, then read quietly through the document. The whole crowd held their breath.

"Marcella," the mayor said. "Please pass me my stamp of approval."

Marcella was already prepared. She handed it over and the mayor stamped the form with a flourish. Then he stood.

"Right, that's that matter dealt with. Now, I believe we've now heard each one of Trevor's legal challenges. They've all been exhausted? There's no other loopholes to exploit?"

He looked at Marcella for affirmation. She nodded.

The mayor continued. "Wonderful. Now we put it to the floor. Does anyone agree with any of these points?" The audience remained completely silent. "And may I have a show of hands for the reinstatement of the sign?" Every single hand went up in the air. "Fabulous," the mayor said, clapping his hands. "In which case I can't see any reason to continue blocking the reinstatement of this sign. Miss Mitchell filled in the paperwork correctly, Mr. Mann has raised issue with everything now I believe he legally can, and there is unanimous agreement amongst the residents that the permit can be granted." He looked over at Marcella again. "Is that it? Have we ticked every one of your ridiculous boxes?"

Marcella pursed her lips and nodded.

"In which case, Emily's sign is reinstated," Mayor Hansen cried, hammering his gavel on the stand. "Meeting dismissed!"

A huge cheer went up in the crowd. Trevor's mouth opened in rage. But he had nothing left to say. He stormed out of the meeting, his fists clenched tightly at his side.

Emily felt elated for the first time in a long time. With her sign back, she'd be certain to get more guests. Her future with the B&B would no longer be precarious. She'd found her footing. Her roots had been planted.

Karen came over and hugged her. "I knew you'd win," she exclaimed. "I think Marcella and Trevor ended up shooting themselves in the foot with all the legal rigmarole, don't you?"

"Seems that way," Emily replied, hugging her back. "Thanks for all your help."

Karen pulled out of the embrace. "I'm just sorry it took so long. But I suppose that doesn't matter now. You kept the B&B afloat in spite of it, and now you can look forward to taking regular bookings."

At those words, Emily felt her happiness begin to diminish. All this time she'd wanted nothing more than to save the B&B. But it had all happened too late. Her enthusiasm had been chipped away by weeks of hardship. Her drive and willpower were waning day by day. And then Amy and Jayne had turned up, just at her lowest point, and offered her an easy way out. Would it be madness to pass them up on their offer? And if she did take it up, what did that mean about Daniel? She knew she shouldn't be with him if he even did show up, but at the same time she didn't know whether she'd even have a choice in the matter; if he did come back to her would her heart demand they reconcile even if her brain knew it wasn't a good idea? And if there were such a possibility, should she get out of Sunset Harbor before she saw him and lost the ability to think rationally?

*

She drove home, her heart beating with anticipation the whole way, wondering if there'd be any signs of Daniel's return. But as she pulled up the driveway, the carriage house remained in darkness and there was no truck in the drive.

She went inside and found Amy and Jayne in their pajamas in the kitchen eating eggs and toast.

"How was your meeting?" Amy asked.

"Great," Emily replied. "I got my sign back."

Jayne raised an eyebrow. "You went to a meeting about a sign?"

Emily shot her a withering glare. "Yes. I did. And I was granted the permit."

"We're really happy for you," Amy said, kicking Jayne under the breakfast bar.

"Of course we're happy for her!" Jayne cried. "I'm just saying that getting up on a Saturday morning to attend a meeting about a sign isn't exactly the most thrilling of activities. Jeez."

"What time is everyone arriving here?" Amy asked, clearly trying to get the conversation back to safer territory.

"About seven p.m.," Emily said. "The ceremony is down by the sea. Then they're coming up here for the party and to sleep over."

"You're remarkably calm," Amy noted.

Emily thought about why that might be for a moment. Was the anticipation of Daniel's return (or failure to return) preventing her from worrying about the wedding party, as though her brain only had so much space with which to worry? Or was it that she had done this before, that she was more confident, more able, this time around?

"I guess," she said. "All the hard work's been done now. The bedrooms are ready. I have a cleaner, a receptionist, a cook. There's not that much for me to do anymore."

Her own words repeated in her mind. Had she taken the B&B as far as it was going to go? There was next to no renovation left to do, no tasks she needed to complete. She wondered if there was even the possibility of the B&B running without her even being here.

"We should go out," Amy said. "Get brunch in town."

"We just had breakfast," Jayne said, gesturing to their empty plates.

"But Emily hasn't. And I'd kill for a Bloody Mary."

"I don't think Joe knows what a Bloody Mary is," Emily said. "But yeah, let's do it. Better than sitting around here all day."

They went out and climbed into Emily's car. She couldn't help but look over at Daniel's empty carriage house as she drove past. It was still early, but the day seemed to be sifting away from her like sand. With each second that passed, her faith in Daniel's return faltered ever so slightly more.

As she drove along the Sunset Harbor streets, Emily noticed the fancy cars and horse-drawn carriages that must belong to the wedding party. It was clearly going to be quite a lavish affair. She felt excited knowing that her little B&B was going to become a part of it but there was also a pang of jealousy in her breast. Other people seemed to have such happy lives, filled with joy and contentment, whereas hers seemed to be filled with anguish.

"Hey, look," Jayne said. "Is that the ceremony taking place down on the beach?"

Emily looked over and saw chairs laid out, the white ribbons blowing in the gentle breeze. It looked beautiful. It looked perfect. She couldn't help but picture herself there standing side by side with Daniel, knowing that such a scenario was probably never ever going to happen. Not with Daniel, anyway. It could always happen with Ben.

Over waffles and coffee, the three friends watched the ceremony taking place on the beach.

No one said a word as Emily's tears began to silently fall. They just reached out and held her hands.

CHAPTER TWENTY NINE

After brunch, Emily, Amy, and Jayne drove back up to the house. Once again, the familiar sight of Daniel's empty driveway greeted Emily.

There were only a few hours left before the wedding party would begin to arrive and the B&B would once again become a hive of activity.

"Parker!" Emily called to the young chef when she caught sight of him out the back. "These are my friends Amy and Jayne."

"That's very nice, Emily. But I have a ton of salads to toss." He rushed off.

"Ooh, Serena!" Emily called next, dragging her young friend by the arm out into the corridor. "This is Jayne. This is Amy."

"Hi," Serena said, waving. "It's nice to meet you. But you're checking out, right? Like, within the next ten minutes? Because we have a full house tonight and I have to make up your bedrooms."

Amy and Jayne looked at Emily.

"I think we should take this as our cue to leave," Amy said.

"Yeah, it's getting a bit hectic," Emily replied. "I'm sorry I didn't have more time for you to stay longer."

"That's cool," Jayne said. "One night in Sunset Harbor is plenty for me. I'm ready to get back to the city."

Emily shot her a look and Jayne held up her hands.

"Just joking," she said with a grin.

They collected their bags and Emily walked with them out to their car.

"You'll think about the job offer?" Amy asked as she got into the driver's seat.

Emily glanced over to the carriage house. "I'll think about it," she said.

She leaned in and kissed Amy's cheek. "Thanks for coming. It was really great to see you. I didn't realize how much I missed you."

Amy patted her hand. "You too, babe. Let's stay in touch this time, okay?"

Emily nodded then went over to the other side of the car and hugged Jayne in the passenger seat.

"I'm sorry if I was a bit brash," Jayne said. "It's just because I love you and it's so strange for me seeing you in a place like this."

"It's part of who I am," Emily replied. "It always has been. Ever since I was a little girl."

"I know. It's just weird. But I'm sorry. I didn't mean to offend you." She smiled a pained smile. It took a lot for Jayne to apologize. Which was probably why she said her next statement in such a huge rush. "And I'm sorry about the whole Ben thing. He was just so pathetic and when I told him I was seeing you he made me tell him where you were! I didn't know he was going to drive up here."

Emily raised one eyebrow at her. "Maybe one day you'll learn how to keep your mouth shut, Jayne," she said.

"I'm really glad you got your sign back, or whatever it was that meeting was about," Jayne added.

Emily couldn't help but laugh, touched that Jayne was at least making the effort. "Thanks, Jayne," she said, shutting the passenger door.

She watched as Amy started up the engine, then she waved as they drove off down the driveway.

She went back inside the B&B to do a final check over everything. It always made her feel proud to see the place in full swing, with people bustling in and out. She was at her happiest when the house was full of laughter and joy.

The first wedding cars arrived not long after Amy and Jayne had left. Emily personally greeted each of the guests, and with Serena's help, everyone was checked in and had congregated in the ballroom, where the live swing band was already playing.

Everyone seemed to be having a great time as they waited for the bride and groom to arrive, but Emily found herself fighting to keep her emotions in check. She decided to head back out through the small door that connected the ballroom to the dining room, which was where all the champagne was laid out for the guests. No one had made a start on the alcohol yet since it was rather early, but Emily did find one person inside clutching a glass. The bride.

"Oh, you've finished with the wedding photographs," Emily said. "Did they go well?"

At first the bride didn't respond and Emily wasn't sure whether she'd heard her or not. She seemed to be transfixed by the painting on the wall, and Emily noticed then that she was crying.

"Is everything okay?" Emily asked, her mind running through a hundred possible scenarios, from the innocent overwhelmed-and-slightly-drunk to the awful already-getting-a-divorce. "Can I get you anything?"

The bride sniffed and shook her head. Then, finally, she turned her tear-stained face toward Emily.

"This painting…" she said, but she didn't finish her words because she was consumed once again by her tears.

Emily walked to her side and looked at the lighthouse painting—the one depicting a nighttime scene that she had given Serena permission to hang.

"I suppose it is a little gloomy," she said, gently.

The bride laughed. "That's not it," she said. She swallowed and finally seemed to find her voice. "You might not believe it, but my mom painted it."

Emily's eyes widened. The news was such a shock to her she had to bite her tongue to keep from screaming. She had a million questions racing through her mind. What if this woman knew something that might answer the mystery of her father's disappearance? She desperately wanted to grill the bride but had to accept that now wasn't the time.

"Really?" she said, keeping her tone measured and even. "My dad was a huge fan. He owned so many of these paintings. I've found at least three in this house, and we had one up in the hallway when I was a kid."

The bride listened to Emily speak, her eyes glassy with tears. "My mom passed away many years ago."

"I'm sorry to hear that," Emily said, touching her lightly on the arm. "I lost one of my parents too."

She didn't mention that her father was technically a missing person; it didn't seem appropriate to bring it up. But her mind was ticking overtime at the possibility that a piece of the puzzle of her life may have been found; that perhaps the death of the artist was linked in some way to the disappearance of her father. If they were lovers, that might explain why he left. She herself understood the agony of losing the person you loved—it cleaved life into two parts, the before and the after, and was so emotionally draining that just waking up in the morning became a struggle.

The bride wiped her tears away. "I'm sorry for the meltdown," she said to Emily. "I was just so taken aback by seeing it."

"It's fine," Emily said. "It's your wedding. You can cry if you want to." She smiled kindly. "Would you like me to take it down?"

"Take it down?" the bride exclaimed. "Goodness no! I feel like it's a sign. Like she is watching me from above. It makes me feel like she's with me."

Emily felt a lump form in her throat. She nodded, then turned her attention back to the painting. They both stood there quietly looking at the painting together.

"Would you like to take one of the pictures?" Emily asked.

The bride looked astonished. "I'm sorry, what?"

Emily shrugged. "It would clearly mean more to you than me. Here, wait one moment."

Emily left the room and went up to her bedroom. In the bedside table drawer she still had the folded up diamond certificate with the lighthouse sketch on the back. She would never know whether it was drawn specifically for her father, or whether he just found it in some flea market like many of his antiques, but really it didn't matter. It would mean so much to the bride, and bring so much more joy to her than it ever could sitting in Emily's drawer.

"Here," Emily said, handing the slip of paper to the bride.

The woman looked at the picture, a small, sad smile on her lips. "I've never seen this before. It's not included in her catalogue." Then she turned it over and her eyes widened with astonishment. "This is... oh my goodness."

"Oh yeah," Emily said. "I found the picture with a diamond of mine and assumed it was the certificate but they must have gotten mixed up somehow as the specifications don't match."

"Because it's the certificate for this diamond," the bride said, holding up her ring. "My mom died of cancer," she explained, her voice cracking. "It was a long battle. She had plenty of time to think about her passing. And so she had this ring made for me for when I got married. There was supposed to be a certificate but no one could ever find it. I just assumed it had gotten lost over the years." Her eyes were wide and grateful.

Emily could hardly believe it. "I don't know what to say. I have no idea how my father came to be in possession of the certificate for it. Do you think there might be a chance that it was accidentally sent to a flea market stall or an antiques store? My dad loved going to those places and if he saw the picture he would definitely have bought it, seeing as he was clearly such a fan."

"Perhaps," the bride said. She gripped the paper tightly. "Thank you so, so much," she whispered. "I'll treasure this forever."

"What was your mother's name, if you don't mind my asking?" Emily said finally. "I couldn't read the signature."

"Antonia Westerly," the bride said. "I'm Catherine Westerly." Then she held up her ring finger, the diamond glinting on the band. "Although it's actually Catherine Jameson now." She smiled.

Emily smiled and pressed her lips together. She was going to ask nothing more of the bride. She would be thankful for this small piece of information. She may be barking entirely up the wrong tree, but every scrap of knowledge brought her closer to understanding. Now she had a name, Antonia Westerly, and that was one lead she could pursue to see where it took her. Emily had a thousand questions burning in her mind, but held her tongue. She didn't want to grill the bride, especially not today of all days, and not when she was already upset. She had to accept that the mystery of her father would not be solved any time soon. If there were answers to be found, she would just have to be patient and wait for fate to give her clues.

The bride finally turned to Emily. She wiped her tears from her eyes. "I think I'm ready to dance now. How do I look?"

Emily looked her up and down. From her gorgeous blond hair swept up onto her head and fastened with pearl bobby pins, to her white lace and silk dress, she looked stunning.

"You look beautiful," Emily said, smiling. "The ballroom's right this way."

CHAPTER THIRTY

The wedding reception went on well into the night. Emily watched, delighted, as Catherine danced the night away. She was clearly having the best night of her life and Emily couldn't help but wonder whether she'd made a mistake by giving Ben such a resounding no. This wedding was everything she'd dreamed of. But when she closed her eyes and tried to picture it being her own wedding, there was only one man she could see in the place of the groom. It was too painful to think like that and so Emily tried her best to force the thoughts from her mind.

But as the clock passed midnight, Emily couldn't help but think about how Daniel hadn't returned. She should have been relieved to know he hadn't walked out on his daughter for her, but she wasn't. She was quietly, selfishly devastated.

Emily stayed up supervising the party until the last guests tumbled into bed. Then quietness descended over the house. The B&B had never been more full and yet Emily had never felt so alone.

She walked back through the house, looking at each room she passed through, each one seeped in memories of happier times with Daniel. Despite everything, the house still had the ability to calm and comfort her. It was like a friend, dependable and reliable.

Emily opened the front door and looked up at the dark, starlit sky. The first cold winds of fall blew around her. Soon the leaves would turn orange and red and transform the landscape into something new. She shivered and grabbed a blanket from the lounge, wrapping it around her shoulders. As she stood on the porch, she felt the urge to walk down to the beach. Something about the chill in the air reminded her of the first time she'd arrived in Sunset Harbor, and of how she'd been drawn here by the ocean. She wanted to see it again now, and feel its calming effect on her.

She walked quietly down the gravel path, illuminated by splotches of light coming from the few bedroom windows that still had their lights on. Then she crossed the street and parted the shrubbery where the foot-trampled path led down to the beach. She followed the path, noticing the chill in the air.

When she reached the ocean, it looked like black tar, reflecting the enormous, inky sky. The waves were very shallow and steady, as though the ocean were sleeping and breathing slowly in and out.

Emily kicked her shoes off and felt the cold sand beneath her toes. She could have stayed like that forever in that moment, in that place of nothing, caught between the before and the after. But she knew she couldn't. She knew at some point she would have to do something, set something into motion.

She took out her cell phone and fired off a quick text to Amy asking if she was still awake. Right away her phone began to ring, with Amy's name flashing on the screen.

Emily answered the call. "Hey."

"Hey, sweetie," Amy said. "Is everything okay?"

"Yeah," Emily said, feeling warmth spread through her at the sound of Amy's voice, feeling her loneliness begin to melt away. "I was thinking about the job offer."

"Yeah?" Amy said, in a tone that obviously was trying to convey nonchalance but was doing anything but.

Emily took a deep breath. "I'm going to take it," she said decisively.

"You are?" Amy cried, a squeal in her voice.

"Yes, I am," Emily said. "I don't think there's any more for me here. I think I've gotten out of this place everything I wanted."

"I'm so happy," Amy said, the delight in her voice audible.

"So am I," Emily said. "And Amy, thanks for not giving up on me at any point over the last few months. I haven't exactly been a good friend."

"That's okay," Amy said. "You're amazing compared to Jayne. We can put it all behind us now. When are you coming back?"

Emily sighed. "Just as soon as I've found a buyer for the B&B, I guess. I'm NOT going to sell it to Trevor. I want it to go to someone local. Someone who will love it like I do."

"Well, the job will be here waiting for you when you're ready, okay?" Amy said.

"Okay," Emily replied.

They ended the call and Emily shivered. The fall wind was chilly. She decided to head back to the house and get some much needed rest.

She walked back across the beach and up the pathway to the road, feeling the gritty sand in her shoes. When she reached the driveway of the inn, she noticed one of the guests was on the porch. In the darkness she couldn't make out what they were doing; it looked like they were fiddling with the hanging baskets. She sighed. It was probably one of the drunk groomsmen thinking it would be hilarious to steal the shrubbery.

She walked closer, ready to chastise him, then stopped in her tracks. It was not one of the wedding party at all, Emily realized with surprise. It was Daniel. Her heart began to race. Her throat seemed to tighten and all the air rushed from her lungs.

"What are you doing?" Emily managed to stammer.

Daniel stopped what he was doing and turned his head over his shoulder. Emily saw then that he had been hanging her sign. It was now in place, hanging proudly above the doorway where it belonged.

"I told you I'd be back before summer ended," Daniel said.

Daniel climbed down the little stepladder and faced her. With her heart beating wildly, Emily slowly approached. It was as though she were approaching an apparition. She paused a little distance away, further than they would normally stand. There was a new stiltedness between them. Emily felt torn. Part of her wanted to throw her arms around him, but another part told her to hold back, that Daniel had changed, that he may not be a man she could trust anymore.

"Are you going to tell me about it?" Emily asked. The question seemed wholly inadequate; as if there were any way he could possibly sum up the last six weeks of his life in his new role as a father.

"Sure," Daniel said. "But I want to show you something first."

Emily frowned. The rational part of her was telling her to go back into the house, but her heart seemed to think that if she followed Daniel there would be something he could do or say that would fix everything between them. It seemed impossible to argue with her heart. She followed Daniel.

He led her along the path. The scene Emily had been hoping to see for six weeks suddenly opened up before her—of the carriage house with Daniel's truck in the drive, filling that horrible empty space that had been taunting her.

"Take a look," Daniel said, gesturing to the truck.

Emily frowned again, more bemused than ever. She couldn't fathom what on earth there could be in the world that would make everything okay, but by the excited look on Daniel's face, he seemed to think it would.

Emily peered in through the back window and gasped. She drew back, her hand over her mouth.

"I didn't want to wake her," Daniel said.

The little girl asleep in the back seat of the car was the most beautiful child Emily had ever beheld. She looked so fragile, so innocent. Her heart melted at the sight of her.

"Is that—"

"My daughter," Daniel replied. "Charlie."

Emily finally looked back at Daniel. Of every scenario she'd imagined, this was not one she'd envisioned. She'd thought there were only two possible outcomes and neither of them ended happily. But this one, this new one that Daniel had managed to conjure, what ending could it bring them? Could there be a way to salvage their relationship in this scenario?

"How?" Emily whispered. Her voice was failing her now as tears choked her. "How did you bring her home with you?"

"I couldn't leave her there," Daniel said. "You were right. Once I was there, there was no way I was walking out on that little girl."

Emily nodded. It had been what she wanted. She couldn't love the version of Daniel that walked out on his child, no matter how inconvenient her existence was.

"But Sheila?" she asked. "Doesn't her mom want to keep her?"

Daniel shook her head. "Sheila was never there, Emily. I saw her once or twice the whole time. She knows she can't care for Charlie properly at the moment. She let me take her home with me."

Emily took a deep breath. Everything was beginning to feel very surreal. She wondered if she was dreaming this whole thing.

"And she's going to live here?" she stated with a nod. "In Sunset Harbor?"

She didn't need Daniel to answer because the answer was so obvious, so clear, as to be as transparent as a diamond. This was the outcome she hadn't allowed herself to consider. Her subconscious had sabotaged her, had hidden from her the one happy ending she longed for. She hadn't let herself entertain the thought for even a second that Daniel would return with the child she craved.

But Daniel did answer. "Yes."

Emily couldn't hold herself back any longer. Six weeks of misery disappeared in one second. She grasped at Daniel, clutched for him, and in an instant their bodies were pressed together tightly. Daniel's mouth opened to hers willingly, so willingly, like he had been craving her all this time as much as she had him.

When they finally broke apart, Emily felt tears running down her cheeks. Daniel's eyes glittered in the starlight.

"I can't believe it," she said, grinning. "You really did come back."

"I could never leave you, Emily," Daniel said.

Just then the little girl stirred awake. Her face was all puffy from sleep, her eyes bleary and red. Whether it was her age or her wavy blond hair, Emily couldn't help but think she bore a striking resemble to Charlotte. Not for the first time since coming to Sunset Harbor, Emily felt as though she was receiving a sign from her deceased sister, that perhaps her sister's spirit was here.

Charlie peered out the window. When she saw Daniel, a huge grin spread across her face. Emily had never seen such a look of pure love.

Daniel opened the back door. "Hey, sweetie. I didn't mean to wake you." He reached in and took the girl out in a way so tender and gentle it melted Emily's heart.

The little girl wrapped her legs around Daniel's waist and let her head drop onto his shoulder. Emily remembered her own father holding her the same way and felt herself fill with warmth at the memory.

"This is Emily," Daniel said, swirling around so that the little girl could see her.

"Hey," Emily said in a quiet, gentle voice.

"Hi," Charlie said shyly, before hiding her head in the crook of Daniel's neck.

"I think she's still a bit sleepy," Daniel said. "I should get her to bed."

Emily nodded. Daniel took a few steps toward the carriage house, and then turned back to Emily.

"Aren't you coming?"

Emily stood there, momentarily paralyzed. Not through fear or worry, but from disbelief that this moment was real. That everything had aligned in her life and settled on this perfect configuration.

"Sure," she said.

She glanced back at the B&B, its sign now hanging proudly above the door, all the lights now extinguished. It looked fantastic, stunning, a true feat. She had made something she was truly proud of. Then she looked back through the open door of the carriage house, no longer in darkness, now lit with the warm glow of lamplight. She watched Daniel move inside as he took the beautiful child in his arms to the bedroom.

She grabbed her cell phone and quickly texted Amy.

I'm sorry. I've changed my mind. I'm staying in Maine.

She walked slowly, knowing that walking through that doorway would mean so much more than that. It would mean a new life, a life richer and scarier than any she had ever imagined. A life filled with more love and unknowns than she could ever imagine. A life that, once she stepped into it, she could never step back out of.

She followed them and paused on the threshold, invited by the warm glow inside.

She breathed the air of the crisp summer night, already feeling fall coming, feeling a change that no one could stop.

And as she took one last deep breath, she stepped inside.

COMING SOON!

FOREVER, WITH YOU
(The Inn at Sunset Harbor—Book 3)

"Sophie Love's ability to impart magic to her readers is exquisitely wrought in powerfully evocative phrases and descriptions....This is the perfect romance or beach read, with a difference: its enthusiasm and beautiful descriptions offer an unexpected attention to the complexity of not just evolving love, but evolving psyches. It's a delightful recommendation for romance readers looking for a touch more complexity from their romance reads."
--*Midwest Book Review* (Diane Donovan re *For Now and Forever*)

"A very well written novel, describing the struggle of a woman (Emily) to find her true identity. The author did an amazing job with the creation of the characters and her description of the environment. The romance is there, but not overdosed. Kudos to the author for this amazing start of a series that promises to be very entertaining."
--*Books and Movies Reviews*, Roberto Mattos (re *For Now and Forever*)

FOREVER, WITH YOU is book #3 in the romance series THE INN AT SUNSET HARBOR, which begins with book #1, FOR NOW AND FOREVER—a free download!

35 year old Emily Mitchell has fled her job, apartment and ex-boyfriend in New York City for her father's abandoned home on the coast of Maine, needing a change in her life. Tapping her life savings to restore the historic home, and with a budding relationship with the caretaker, Daniel, Emily prepares to open the Inn at Sunset Harbor as Memorial Day comes.

But all does not go as planned. Emily learns quickly that she has no idea how to run a B&B. The house, despite her efforts, needs new, urgent repairs she cannot afford. Her covetous neighbor is still determined to make trouble for her. And worst of all: just as her relationship with Daniel is blossoming, she learns he has a secret. One which will change everything.

With her friends urging her to return to New York City and her ex-boyfriend trying to win her back, Emily has a life-changing decision to make. Will she try to stick it out, to embrace small-town life, her father's old house? Or will she turn her back on her new friends, neighbors and life—and on the man she has fallen in love with?

FOREVER, WITH YOU is book #3 of a dazzling new romance series that will make you laugh, make you cry, will keep you turning pages late into the night—and will make you fall in love with romance all over again.

Book #4 will be available soon.

Sophie Love

A lifelong fan of the romance genre, Sophie Love is thrilled to release her debut romance series, which begins with FOR NOW AND FOREVER (THE INN AT SUNSET HARBOR—BOOK 1)

Sophie would love to hear from you, so please visit www.sophieloveauthor.com to email her, to join the mailing list, to receive free ebooks, to hear the latest news, and to stay in touch!